BROKEN
arrow

D1599459

www.chellebliss.com

CHELLE BLISS

USA TODAY BESTSELLING AUTHOR

COPYRIGHT

OPEN ROAD SERIES

Book 1 - Broken Sparrow (Morris)
Book 2 - Broken Dove (Leo)
Book 3 - Broken Wings (Crow)
Book 4 - Broken Arrow (Arrow)

The Open Road series is interconnected with the Men of Inked: Heatwave series. Learn more at menofinked. com/heatwave-series

Also available with discreet covers

CHAPTER 1
ANNIE

"ANNIE, MAY I HAVE A WORD?"

The hairs on the back of my neck rise at the sound of her voice, but even worse are her five-inch heels spiking their way across the linoleum floor.

I turn quickly, my long ponytail whipping against my bare shoulders, and put on a bright, fake smile. "Hey there, June. Hi. Of course."

June stomps through the studio lobby with her aviators pulled down as if all the glass in the lobby is letting in far too much sun. And to be fair, it kind of is.

I loop the backpack that's been hanging off one shoulder over both my arms and secure it on my back, mostly so I have something to do with my hands. I grip the straps and rock back and forth on my heels. "Is there something you need?" I ask, anxious to get up to my studio.

June extends a hand toward me. "As a matter of fact, I have something I think you might need."

I squint at what she's holding and immediately

recognize the colorful lanyard. It's mine. At the sight of it, I swing the backpack off my back and check the zipper. Neither the lanyard nor the carabiner clip I use to fasten my keys and ID to my bag are there.

Instead of feeling grateful that she found it, I feel my tummy drop at the reality that they were missing and I didn't even know it.

Without it, I might have been locked outside of someplace I wanted to get in. And the way things have been the last few weeks, the idea that I might be outside needing to get in someplace and not be able to… I feel almost dizzy at the thought.

I swallow hard and try not to let her know that this is in any way a big deal. "Oh wow. Thanks. I would have missed these when I got upstairs and couldn't get into my studio." I take the lanyard and keys from her. "Where, uh, where did you find them?"

June pushes up her sunglasses, using them to hold her severe black bob away from her face. She purses her perfect red lips and waves a hand at me dismissively. "A custodian found them and saw you were a grad student. He brought them to me, and now I'm giving them back to you." She turns to walk away but singsongs as she leaves, "You're welcome."

"Thank you," I mumble again under my breath, not sure if I should be grateful for her help or worried about where my ID was all the time I didn't notice it was missing.

I'd skipped breakfast in the cafeteria, but I'd grabbed a coffee and swiped my card then.

After getting coffee, I'd drunk it by the fountain and

talked to my dad. Then I'd run off campus to a local thrift shop. I'd left my backpack in the car and just brought in my wallet and phone. At worst, my ID and keys had been floating around campus for half the morning. Where anyone could have found them and done anything to them.

Shit.

Just as my mood starts to go from worried to pissed, I remind myself to focus on the positive.

A custodian found them and turned them in to the one person who would know where to find me and return them. I should be grateful June took the time to bring everything to me.

As soon as I'm in my studio, I'll log in to my student account and make sure nobody went on a shopping spree. If the custodian found them right away, I'm sure everything is fine.

Everything has to be fine.

Unless it isn't.

In which case, my already shit month is about to get a lot more complicated.

Today should've been a normal day for me, too.

I've got the opportunity of a damned lifetime.

I'm in the grad program of my dreams. I'm being trained for a career that most people could only dream of. A career that until about eight weeks ago, even I could only dream of.

I take a nice deep breath and thank my lucky stars that my dad finally had a change of heart. Two months ago, I was half asleep, answering phones at the law offices of Hancock & Engler. My dad is Ellis Hancock.

I was only nine when Dad decided to pick himself up and get over the loss of my mom.

Hell. We'll never get over losing her. He knows that. I know it.

But we'd been a team, Dad and I, for almost three years, until one day Dad told me that he was going to do something new with his life. Something he never believed he could do, but he'd decided life was far too short to keep dreams tucked away in his back pocket.

We both knew life was far too short. That became crystal clear the day we'd found out Mom wasn't just sick, she was dying.

Dad seemed to give up on life when he lost Mom, but one day, we toured a school that catered to nontraditional students. They had a childcare center on-site, so Dad didn't have to leave me alone.

The day Dad went back to school was the day that changed both of our lives forever.

I'll never forget the day that Amanda Grace, one of the childcare workers, brought in a white trash bag filled with old clothes, buttons, skeins of yarn, and needles and thread.

"What's all this?" I'd asked.

It wasn't always Amanda Grace who watched us, but she is the one I remember best. She was wild and colorful, always wearing homemade clothes and the brightest colors on her fingers and toes.

She was my first real role model other than my dad. And she was the one who made me believe art wasn't just something to stick on the walls. Art was living, breathing, wearable, usable, recyclable, and real.

I was reborn as an aspiring artist. But like most childish dreams, my passion didn't last for long. By the time I was sixteen, I needed a job, and my art wasn't making any money. Dad needed a receptionist, and the rest, as they say, was history.

I went to college but only studied art as a minor. I hadn't fully bought in to my ability to create art and support myself. My degree's in English just in case I ever decide to go to law school like my dad.

I'd thought my life was set in stone. I answered phones for two years after graduating from college. But that all changed this summer. And now, I'm unemployed and pursuing a master's degree at one of the most prestigious private art colleges in the state of Florida.

I should be savoring every second. Soaking up the opportunity. Dreaming of the day when I can sell my work, display in galleries, teach private workshops... But since school started a month ago, nothing, and I mean nothing, has gone the way I expected.

First, things with Dad have been odd, to say the least.

Then there're the notes.

Thinking about them makes the hair on my arms stand on end. I take off down the hall, wanting to get upstairs to my studio, lock the door, and get some work done. And hopefully put some of the weird shit that's been happening lately out of my mind.

But the atmosphere in the Arts Building isn't helping me find my happy place. The slap of my flip-flops against the tile seems to echo too loudly. Like my own shoes are alerting everyone that I'm here.

I'm fine, I think. I'm not alone. I'm safe. Nothing can happen with all these people around. Even with everybody in the classrooms, I'm fine.

I head toward the elevator, but then notice a guy I don't know, hustling like he's hopelessly late for class, blast through the front door. He rushes past me, passing by so close I feel the heat of his body. My heartbeat picks up, and I squeeze my hands into fists. He skids on a well-worn pair of skater shoes up to a closed classroom and starts quietly apologizing to the room for being late.

"See?" I mutter under my breath. "Everything is fine. Just calm down."

But my worry senses won't settle down. Every time I've received one of those weirdo letters, it's happened in this building. Whoever has been leaving the letters for me not only has access to this building when it's open, but they probably know when I'm here.

I can't help the clawing feeling that crawls up the back of my neck as I press the elevator call button.

I'm alone.

But I'm fine.

No one is out to get me.

The notes are stupid.

They're probably pranks.

I won't get another one.

Everything is fine.

I have to believe that.

Weird shit like this happens to people all the time, right? In a few months, this will be a distant memory.

In the meantime, I need to go deep into what I'm here to do.

The ding of the elevator arriving breaks me from my thoughts. I step in and press the button for the second floor, but just as the doors start to close, a hand slips between them.

"Sorry." An older guy walks into the elevator, giving me a tight smile. "Thanks for waiting."

I have no idea who he is or where he came from.

Chill the fuck out, Annie. Nothing is going to happen between the first and second floors. I'll be getting off in a second.

I try to reassure myself, but then the stranger presses the already illuminated button for two, and it hits me.

My floor. He's going to my floor.

There is no way in hell I'm riding up with him. I slip past him and get the heck out of the elevator before the doors have a chance to close again. "Crap. Forgot something. Sorry," I call out, glancing over my shoulder to get another look at the guy.

The man gives me a dark look as the doors close.

I take a ragged breath and hope he's gone when I finally do make it up there.

Alone again, I let my shoulders sag, convinced I'm losing my grip. I can't live like this. Afraid of who's watching me. And, even worse, wondering why. How the hell am I going to get through this semester?

"Annie Hannie. Wait up, babe."

This time, the voice that calls to me makes me feel

instantly at ease, and I chuckle. Only Neveah, the grad-uate resident adviser, would make up such a silly rhyme for my name.

Getting to know people like Neveah is one of the things I love most about being here. She dresses the part, and talking with her makes me feel like the world is beautiful, colorful, and safe, which is exactly how she sees it.

That's how I saw it too—at least until recently.

She marches up to me wearing secondhand men's boots and a flowy patchwork dress that looks like it was cobbled together with scraps from someone's grand-mother's sewing bin. She's got her long, dark curls knotted in a bun. Her bracelets clang against one another as she holds out her arms to me.

"You off to your studio? Take the stairs with me. I ate a boatload of cafeteria French toast and could use the exercise. I'm going to be fighting those carbs for days. Let's burn some bread off these thighs."

He may be up there.

"You okay, cupcake? You look like you just stepped in a turd wearing flip-flops."

I giggle at the comparison, shaking off my paranoia. "No, nothing that bad," I tell Neveah, trying to put a smile on my face. "I'm just anxious to get some work done."

"Same, girl. Same," she says. "If I take any more time to finish that commission…" She whistles between her teeth, the sound echoing sharply through the quiet hall. "Gloomy June is never going to recommend me for paying work again."

I have to chuckle. Our thesis adviser is as gloomy as her hair is dark, but Nevaeh has a decent relationship with the woman. Unlike me. I see every glare and snide remark from June as a personal attack against me. I always get the feeling that she thinks I don't deserve to be here.

And if the notes are to be believed, she's not the only one.

Together, Neveah and I head to the stairwell and take the two flights up to the second floor.

Neveah is fanning her face with a hand by the time we reach the door. "Who needs a gym on this small-ass campus when we get all the cardio we need just taking the stairs."

I grin, not quite as out of breath as she is, but I'm wearing shorts, a tank, and flip-flops, compared to her combat boots, maxi dress, and shawl.

Nevaeh's studio is the closest to the stairwell, so she fumbles in her crocheted purse for the key and lets herself in. "Call me if you need a lunch buddy," she says. "But no more carbs today. Salad buffet or smoothies," she says, disappearing behind the metal door.

I'm already calmer after just a few minutes with Neveah, so I step right over the piece of paper that's been shoved under my door. It's not until I set down my backpack and turn to lock the door behind me that I see it. I immediately recognize the handwriting hastily scrawled on a piece of notebook paper folded in half.

Annie.

My heart nearly stops in my chest when I see it. With trembling fingers and knees shaking so hard I can hardly stand, I bend and pick up the note. I hold it in my fingers like I might get hurt just touching it.

I consider throwing it away. Crumpling it in a tight ball and pitching it in the trash. Anything but reading it and the fucked-up messages I don't understand.

Lighting anything on fire in the studios is prohibited, or I'd find two sticks and rub them together to spark a blaze and burn the note before I have to look at what's inside.

But if I don't read it, I won't know what the hell this person wants. I won't know how much worse it is. Or maybe, how much better? How long can whoever this is keep up this stupid game?

The question hammers between my ears, and finally, I unfold the paper.

I have to read it.

I have to know.

No matter how much scarier this gets, I have to know.

I know it was you, Annie. I know what you did. The next message will have instructions. Be ready. You're going to pay.

CHAPTER 2
ARROW

CERTAIN PERFUMES ARE MORE criminal than any of the shit my clients get caught up in.

I try to listen to the woman telling me she is certain that her dog walker is trying to poison her with a cheesecake, but all I can do is flare my nostrils and hope I get enough fresh air with every breath that I don't pass out. The scent itself isn't bad, but the amount she's wearing is beyond obscene.

"Mrs. Mangione," I tell her, getting up from behind my desk to come around the front and offer my hand.

"Miss," she corrects. "There hasn't been a Mr. Mangione in my life for over ten years."

Because I'm about twenty years younger than she is and in desperate need of clients, not girlfriends, this woman is off-limits. Besides, one date with Ms. Mangione and I'd end up a casualty of her fragrance. Sadly, I don't think this lady has a promising case or a bulging wallet, so I'm going to politely show her the way out.

She graciously accepts my hand.

"Now, here's what I suggest," I say gently, steering her toward the door of my office.

The sign on my small storefront is new, the brushed aluminum bearing the name of my year-old business:

Arrow Investigations and Security

The sign only cost me a hundred and fifty bucks at some online store, but it classes up the place considerably. I look like a real business, even though most days my clientele is far from the kind that I need to keep that sign legit.

"I'm deathly allergic to cheesecake. Dairy allergy. I haven't touched the stuff since I was a girl. She knows this." She flutters her fake lashes and clutches my arm. "Can you help me?"

I walk her through my tiny lobby and let the bright Florida sunshine blast us with heat. "I absolutely can help you." I accompany her down the sidewalk to the large, colorful shop at the very end of the strip mall. "Come with me."

The entire commercial property is owned by friends of my buddy Leo Hawk. Leo's wife Lia owns the very place we're headed.

"What is this?" Ms. Mangione covers her overdrawn lips with her hands. "How adorable!"

I activate the automatic entry, then step aside to let the lady through. The sounds of happy barking and some not-so-happy growling greet us as we enter the doggie day care and grooming facility.

An enormous man is behind the counter, huffing and looking at a mounted iPad like the thing is toxic.

"Tiny?" I ask, confused at seeing him here. "Where's Lia?"

The man's nickname is perfectly suited to his far-from-tiny size. He's the president of the Disciples motorcycle club, and with his leather vest and short-sleeve Harley T-shirt underneath, he is literally the last person I expect to see working behind the counter. Except his expression right now truly does give off mad dog vibes.

Tiny grunts before he flicks a quick glance at me, then Ms. Mangione, and then he ambles to his feet. "Arrow." He says my nickname like he's pissed, but then he softens his tone. "And, ma'am." There is something weird about the way he says that.

I look over at my potential client to see her making the strangest sort of fluttery eye movements at Tiny. "I'm Marla," she drawls, extending a hand across the counter. "Marla Mangione. And you are?"

"My friends call me Tiny," he says, shaking her hand. "That's what you should call me."

Marla laughs like that's the most hilarious thing she's ever heard, and I quickly realize that I've definitely lost this client to this place. Which, I guess, is what I was hoping for anyway.

"Tiny," I explain, "Ms. Mangione is having an issue with her current dog walker."

"That so?" he asks, lowering a brow. "What's the problem? Somebody givin' you a hard time?"

Before Ms. Mangione can answer, a squealing sound comes from behind the counter.

"Up! Up!"

Tiny holds up a finger. "Excuse me, ma'am. My daughter owns this shop here, and her babysitter called in sick today. I'm watching my grandson for a couple hours." Tiny bends down and opens his arms.

Then I watch what's left of Marla Mangione's composure melt away like a dairy freeze in the Florida sun.

"Who do we have here?" she asks.

While Tiny introduces his grandson Rider, Lia comes running in from the back room where she handles the grooming, her hair tied up under a cap, wearing a simple branded blue smock over her clothes.

"I heard my baby." As Lia hustles through the store, a dozen dogs follow her like she's their leader, especially Lia's own dogs—the trio of small dogs she calls her girl crew and her most recent rescue, a male pitty named Mikey. She laughs and looks down at the pups trailing her heels. "Not you, babies. My baby Rider." Lia cocks her head at her father, who is bouncing eighteen-month-old Rider on a knee. "You guys good, Dad?"

Tiny looks like he's better than good. His cheeks are red, and he's blowing raspberries at his grandson like it's his job. Marla Mangione is clutching her enormous knock-off designer purse in her hands and watching the whole scene with a look of rapt adoration.

"Lia," I say, clearing my throat. "This is Marla Mangione. She may need a new…"

But it's obvious no more introductions are needed. Tiny and Marla are talking over the counter about kids and dogs, and Lia crosses her arms over her chest with a look of giddy fascination at her father and son.

"Nice meeting you, Ms. Mangione," I say and turn to leave.

I'm not part of the MC, never have been, so I'm used to feeling like I'm on the outside looking in. They've got it from here, and I left my shop unlocked. We have plenty of cameras and security, but I may as well get back.

Besides, business has been so slow lately, I don't have much more than a badly out-of-date laptop in the place. My business makes an incredibly disappointing mark.

Satisfied that Marla's dog-walking situation didn't require a PI as much as a new doggie day care, I turn and head out.

"Arrow!"

I turn back to see Lia give me a sly smile.

"Thanks, bud." She nods at Marla. "Appreciate the referral."

I nod, then wave a wordless goodbye to Tiny. When I first came back to town, I had a little bit of a flirtation going on with Lia. I mean, who could resist her? She's got that hippie, free-spirited vibe, banging curves, and a personality that doesn't quit. She was living with my buddy Tim's little brother, Leo, but it turned out they were more than just roommates. The former roommates-with-benefits are now parents to little Rider, and I'm happy to have a friend in Leo, who's in the MC.

But friend is a loose term. I'm not part of anything like these guys are. No real family. All my friends are like family to me, but most of them have their own demons. Or, like Leo and Tim, have a club or kids or other demands on their lives.

At least I have a business. It ain't much, but it's all mine. As I head back for another afternoon of doom-scrolling my client list and bank account, a familiar motorcycle is rolling into the lot.

"Yo." I nod at my buddy Leo and slow my steps as he parks his bike in front of his auto shop.

"Hey, bud." He lifts his chin toward my office. "You workin' or playin'?"

"Wishing I had work, man, but I just sent a client over to your girl. Lady needs a dog walker, not a PI."

Leo yanks off his sunglasses and claps me on the shoulder with one hand. In the other, he's carrying a kiddie meal from a local fast-food place. "Thanks. Maybe you should learn to shampoo dogs."

I pretend to throw a punch at my buddy's gut, but I laugh it off. "Kid's getting big," I tell him, motioning toward the doggie day care. "Looks like he's having fun with Gramps in there."

Leo chuckles and scrubs a hand over his chin. "I know, right? The kid's got the appetite of a teenager and is just as stubborn. Lia's begging me to give him a brother or sister, but…" He yanks on the door of the shop where he works with his brother, Tim. "I'm going to need more business too if I'm going to feed more mouths."

"Let's grab dinner soon, yeah?" I ask.

"Definitely," Leo calls behind him as he heads toward his wife's place.

If I know Leo, definitely means someday, and

despite his best intentions, someday isn't likely to happen any time soon. Between his club brothers, his business, and his family, the guy doesn't get a lot of free time.

But it's all good. I've got my own shit to face. If I can't find some more clients who can actually afford to pay me, I'll be giving notice on my lease and moving on.

I yank open the door to my office and breathe a sigh of relief that the scent of Ms. Marla Mangione has been blown away, thanks to the sturdy efforts of my window-mounted AC. I have just stepped foot inside the small lobby when a voice comes out of nowhere.

"Excuse me? I didn't want to startle you. There was no one at the front desk…"

I almost lurch out of my boots at the woman's voice. She's standing off to one side, hidden from view of the street. I look her over, then look behind me. She's alone and looks nervous, scared even.

"Yeah, I'm, uh, short a receptionist at the moment."

That's a mostly true statement. I never had a receptionist, but I optimistically bought the extra furniture when I signed the lease. Too bad I have more optimism than clients.

I close the exterior door to keep the heat of the afternoon out where it belongs, trying not to glare at the woman in my office. She's young, I'd guess, but not much younger than me. Early twenties. She's dressed in super-short white shorts that cling to a deliciously rounded ass. The tank top she's wearing hugs her flat belly, and her tits are on the smaller size but perfectly shaped. Her legs are long, tanned, and toned, and a sandy blond braid falls to the middle of her back.

But it's the backpack slung over both shoulders that makes her look like a college kid. Maybe it's just what she uses as a purse, but the way she's ducking her shoulders means either that backpack is really freaking heavy or she's trying to hide or make herself harder to see. It would be impossible to miss a woman who looks like that, so I'm guessing she's loaded down with textbooks or something. But why exactly she's standing in my office is the bigger question.

"Are you looking for a PI?" I ask on a frown. As pretty as she is to look at, I need to make a few calls to my buddies at a couple of insurance companies that hire me for surveillance. It's been a while since I had any corporate work, and unfortunately, part of this job is networking. If I'm lucky, I'll score a suspected workers' comp fraud case this week. Just one of those would keep the lights on for...fuck. At least a little while longer.

The woman doesn't answer my question but shuffles from flip-flop to flip-flop.

I head toward my office and wave for her to follow me. "Why don't you have a seat? Tell me how I can help."

She glances nervously toward the door, as if she's afraid to trust me. I've learned a lot about body language in my years as a bond agent and even more since I've been working as a private investigator. Whatever's brought the girl in here, she's genuinely uncomfortable.

"Why don't we talk out here?" I motion toward the never-used guest chair in front of the reception desk.

There's really no need for us to meet in my office. It's all the same anyway. There's nothing on my desk but an underused laptop. Out here, there's a big, blocky desk calendar that's four months out of date. I never meet with people out here, so while the girl pulls out a chair and sits across from me, I tear off the sheets and crumple them up, then stuff them in the empty bin beside the desk.

With that done, I lean back in the seat and look through the empty desk drawers for a pen. Shit, there's nothing in here. Instead of taking notes or completing an intake form, I'll have to sit here and just listen, which is probably going to make her feel even more awkward.

"Let me grab a pen," I say, jumping up from behind the desk. "You want a water or something?" Her obvious discomfort is starting to make me feel sweaty, so I pop open the tiny fridge beside my desk and grab two bottles of cold water. Then I snag a pen from the top of my desk and an unused pad of lined paper.

When I head back into the tiny lobby space, the blond woman is squinting at me, twisting around in her seat to look me over. She's still got the backpack over her shoulders and has her ass perched on the edge of the chair like any minute she might change her mind and run out of here.

"Here you go," I say, setting the water bottle on the desk in front of her. I drop the notepad on my side of the desk, tuck the pen behind my ear, uncap my water, and take a big swallow.

Much better.

When I sit back down, she still hasn't said anything, so I give her a look. "So, you know I'm a private investigator, right? Are you looking to hire someone?"

She glances back at the door as if checking the sign to be sure she's in the right place. "What about security?" she asks. "Do you also offer security services?"

I take another quick swig of ice-cold water and nod. "Yeah, I do." I narrow my eyes and cross my arms over my chest. "Why don't we start with the basics? I'm Josh, but people call me Arrow. And your name is?"

She looks at my crossed arms, then extends her hand. "Anne Hancock, but people call me Annie."

I can see that the white polish on the hand she holds out to me is far from fresh. The chips left on her nails look old, like she hasn't had them done in weeks.

She's waiting for me to shake her hand, but the pale blue of her eyes is so unusual, so stunning against her tanned skin, I feel a buzz of attraction all the way down to my balls. Touching her may not be the best idea, but I can't exactly refuse to shake the woman's hand. I clasp her hand quickly and then release.

"Nice to meet you, Annie," I say. "What brings you in today?" I try to sound a little more formal, taking a professional approach with my brain while my body is having a far less professional reaction to Annie Hancock.

What she says next, though, shifts the mood in the room immediately. "I...I think I am in some kind of trouble. But I'm not sure."

"You think you're in trouble?" I echo, scribbling

absolute nonsense on my legal pad, just to give me something to focus on that's not the long lines of Annie Hancock's neck. "So, what's going on?"

She swallows hard, and I see her look at the bottle of water like it might be poisoned. She picks it up carefully and gently twists the cap, not strong enough to break the safety seal, though. She's tugging it just lightly enough to ensure that the water is, in fact, sealed and hasn't been tampered with.

Something deep in my gut reacts immediately. Whatever is going on for this girl, she's afraid. She's hyperaware of her surroundings. Checking that a bottle of water hasn't been tampered with. While I wasn't too concerned that Ms. Mangione's dog walker was really trying to poison her with cheesecake, whatever is going on with Annie Hancock feels real and serious.

I don't know this woman, but I want to know just what happened to make her so terrified for her safety that she's checking the caps on bottled water.

"Let's cut to it," I say gruffly, anxious to get to her story. "Did something happen? Do you think you're in danger?"

She presses her full lips together and looks down at her hands. She's fiddling with the cap on the water bottle, but she hasn't taken a sip yet. Suddenly, I'm worried, angry, and almost out of patience.

"Look," I say, lifting my brows and pointing at the water. "You're safe with me, Annie. I haven't tampered with the water bottle. I'll pour some into a cup and drink it myself if it'll make you feel better. Now, if you're thirsty, go ahead and take a sip so you can get on with it. Because unless I know nothing about reading people, you're scared shitless about something. Something big enough to bring you into my office. And I'd really like to figure out if I can do anything to help you."

A flush blooms like a cloud from her perfect cleavage up along her collarbone. She lowers her eyes and sighs. "You're not like the others," she murmurs, a slight smile lightening her dark expression.

"The others?" I ask.

She nods. "You're the third stop I've made today. The other investigators weren't so caring."

Well, that's a first. Even when I do my job and catch the cheating spouses in the act or grab evidence that can help an insurance carrier deny a fraudulent claim, I'm not often given a warm handshake and a hearty thank-you. I've been called every insult in the book at least a hundred times, and usually the insults are smothered in curses.

As I look over Annie, I can only imagine what the other PIs put her through. "Lemme guess," I say, snorting air and trying not to swear. "They didn't ask any questions but wanted an up-front deposit for their time, plus expenses. That, or they tried to hit on you and told you it was all in your head."

She looks me in the eye, strength in her gaze. "Yeah. You're exactly right. But you seem…different."

I may not have earned her trust yet, but after she says the words, she takes a long sip of water. I watch the tiny hairs on her arms lift up and her nipples peak hard against her tank.

"So," I say roughly, clearing my throat and tearing my eyes from her cleavage. "I'm here to listen. Maybe even help. What's the problem? Jealous boyfriend? Roommate trouble?"

She sets the water down and scoots the chair a little closer to the desk. "No, no, nothing like that. I think…" She smooths her hands along her hair. The stray loose strands stick in place, giving me a perfect view of her face as she says, "I think maybe someone wants to blackmail me."

After years of working with people from the darkest corners, I am hardly surprised by much. But I am skeptical. I've managed to stay in business because people do shady, shady shit. They steal from one another, they lie… Even blood. Families turn on one another for the stupidest fucking reasons. But so far, all I have is a scared-looking woman and a name. I'm going to need a hell of a lot more to know whether I'm talking to a client or wasting my time.

"So, tell me," I press. "Do you have enemies? Somebody you crossed?"

She shakes her head. "That's just the thing. My life is boring. I don't know why anyone would want to do this to me." She bites down on her lower lip, as if she's hesitating to tell me the whole story.

"Do what to you, Annie?" I ask. "Look, I can't help you if I don't know what's going on. Even if you do tell me everything, this might be a police matter. But you've got to give me details. Even if it's uncomfortable. You wouldn't be the first person to send pictures of an intimate nature to someone and later regret it. Am I right? Is it something like that?"

To my shock, she laughs. A light, free-sounding laugh that brightens her entire face. "God, no." She shakes her head. "My father is a lawyer, and I'm twenty-five, Mr. Arrow. I know better than to send naked pictures of myself to people I date."

The thought of her posing for pictures like that brings another blast of very unprofessional feelings, so I picture pouring that bottle of ice water over my head and cooling myself the fuck off. "Okay, great," I say. "So, what details can you share about what's going on?"

She grows serious, worrying that lip again between her teeth, then shrugs the backpack off her shoulder. She sets the thing in her lap and, finally, starts talking. "I'm a grad student," she explains as she works the zipper open. "I wasn't supposed to go to grad school, but about two months ago, my dad told me he didn't want me working in his office anymore. He wanted me to pursue my dreams." She laughs, but the sound is flat, not joyful. "He's never supported my dreams of being an artist before, which was why I was working for him in the first place."

I nod, watching as she reaches a hand inside her backpack. I study her carefully, curious for a second as to whether she's got a weapon in there.

"Hey," I say sharply, nodding at her bag.

She jumps at the edge in my tone and doesn't move.

"You carrying?" I demand. "Anything in there I should be worried about?"

Her shoulders release like tightly wound springs. "Oh God, no. No, sorry. I don't have a gun. Nothing in here like that." She holds up a small fabric pouch. "Needle and thread, some fabric. One pair of really sharp scissors. I'm an artist. Textiles."

I nod for her to continue since I don't think this Annie Hancock is here to exact revenge on behalf of one of my former clients. I watch her body language as she pulls a glossy blue folder from her backpack.

"About two months ago, my dad told me he'd pulled some strings and had gotten me into Mid-Florida College of Fine Arts. That was super weird. Dad has always wanted me to follow in his footsteps and work with him."

"And what's your father's line of work again?" I ask.

"Lawyer," she says. "So, what's weird is that the application period closed months ago. To get into the masters' program, you have to put together a portfolio of work, complete a personal statement, and get letters of recommendation. I didn't do any of that."

That is odd. "Your old man do all that for you? Maybe as a surprise from Daddy?"

"I'm not some spoiled rich kid, Mr. Arrow," she says, the first real grit I've heard in her voice. "My father's a real estate attorney. We're not rolling in money. Far from it."

"But you think he bought your way into grad school? Is that what you're implying?"

She shrugs. "I don't really know. I did have to go through the steps and complete my application, but it was all very late. I got a conditional acceptance letter before I even applied."

"So, you did apply, then?" Something here just ain't adding up. The kid wanted to go to art school, and her dad decided to send her. Sounds simple enough. "Maybe he had a change of heart. A recent health scare. He realized life's too short to force your kid to be a lawyer when she really wants to do…" I already forgot what kind of art she said she does, but she reminds me.

"Textile art." She sniffs lightly and shakes her head. "I wish that were the case," she says. "But I don't think so. I wouldn't have worried about it and would've just thrown myself into the opportunity, but then this happened…"

She slides the glossy blue folder, the kind I used in high school to keep my homework from wrinkling, across the desk to me.

"These letters…" she starts, but then her voice catches. "I thought they were maybe just a mean joke. Maybe someone at school found out I got in around the normal channels and was pranking me. Until this last one."

I open the folder and see several notes handwritten on lined paper tucked into the pockets. "Have you shown these to anyone else?" I ask. "Your father? Any campus security people or anything?"

She shakes her head. "I don't want my father to pull me out of school," she admits. "And I'm afraid if I involve campus security, they'll call my father."

That all sounds reasonable enough if she's getting shitty notes delivered to her. But if she's really worried about her safety, I can't understand why she wouldn't alert anybody and everybody who might be able to sort this out. Her father, the school. The police, if it's serious enough.

"Has anyone else touched these?" I ask. "Just you?"

She looks confused but nods.

"I'm going to grab a pair of gloves. If these ever need to be examined for fingerprints, I'd rather not leave mine behind or destroy what might still be there."

"Oh God." She pales and watches me as I get up and walk into my office to retrieve a standard pair of latex gloves from a supply cabinet. "Do you think it's that serious, Mr. Arrow? I've read and reread these like dozens of times. I've touched them so much that I can't imagine anyone else's prints are on them."

"Call me Josh," I say, sliding on the gloves. "Let's leave that to the experts when and if it goes there. For now, I'm just going to be cautious."

I suppress a groan when I see she hasn't just read them tons of times, she's used a Sharpie and labeled each note with a date and time. All except one.

"This," I say, pointing to the bright-red Sharpie ink. "This is you?"

She nods. "The date and time I found each note. Except the last one. That one came this morning."

I carefully open each note and read them in order.

And after I read the last one, I'm absolutely certain what this woman needs is more than just a strip mall PI. She needs to go to the police.

CHAPTER 3
ANNIE

"THE POLICE?" My heart rate spikes as I repeat the words the private investigator said. "You think this is serious? Do you think I'm really in danger? I was hoping this was just, like, a weird joke."

I start looking frantically around the office for a bathroom. I need to cool off. I feel sick. I need to splash my face, or I'm liable to lose the contents of my stomach. I can't believe this. I might really be in some kind of danger?

"Annie." His voice is kind as he comes around the desk with a worried look on his face. "First of all, I want you to calm down, okay? I want you to take a deep breath and focus with me. You're safe. I want you to remember that. I'm going to keep you safe."

I grab the bottle of water and take another sip. The other private investigators were exactly what I expected. Old. Grizzled. A little creepy. They all just wanted money up front and didn't even listen to what was going on.

Josh is different.

He hasn't asked me for a dime, and already, he's told me more times than anyone ever has that I'm safe. I want so desperately to believe him.

"I need you to do something for me," he says, peeling the latex gloves off from the wrist and then dumping them in the little trash bin beside the desk. Then he goes back to his chair and sits. "Annie?"

I nod and stare into his eyes, waiting for instructions.

He leans forward and puts both hands, palms down, flat on the desk. "Just take a second and take a deep breath in, okay?"

I watch his calm face; the steadiness in his palms seems to ground me in the moment. I relax my hands and take a deep breath.

He gives me a real smile then. Not the professional, distant smile of a man who might just send me out the door when he learns I can't afford a massive retainer. The reassurance on his face feels sincere. Like it's meant just for me.

"A little better?" he asks.

I nod. "Yes, thank you."

"All right. If you feel ready, I want you to tell me everything you can about these notes. How were they delivered? Was there anything unusual that happened right before you started receiving them? Who else knows about them? I'm going to take notes, but I'm paying attention to every detail, so try to remember anything that might be important, even if you're not sure." He holds up those strong hands as if warning me to slow down before I even get started. "But if you need a minute, it's fine. Take all the time you need."

I can't get over the fact that I'm not paying this guy for his time and yet he's doing the actual opposite of rushing me. Maybe I've been around lawyers too long. They bill for every microsecond of their time, and I guess when you've spent tens of thousands or more on your education and many more years perfecting your expertise, then you should charge for your time. But again, Josh isn't like anyone else I've known.

I inhale and catch the softest hint of what I think is Josh's cologne. He seems young for a private investigator. He's got longish brown hair that is parted on one side and sort of swoops over his right eye. As far as I can see, he's got nice blue eyes, and his beard is trimmed. I want to know how scratchy or smooth it is. The feeling seems totally inappropriate given the circumstances, but I've never been in this situation before.

My instincts feel all out of whack. Thinking the investigator guy is hot is a lot better than thinking he's creepy. When he catches me staring at him, another smile lightens the seriousness of his expression, and I smile back. Warmth spreads through my belly, and I start to feel calmer.

"You good?" he asks.

I nod, and I mean it. I am better.

So, I tell this handsome stranger exactly how I found the notes—each one slipped under the door of my private studio at school. He asks a bunch of questions— who has keys to the studio, is my schedule the same every day, have I ever seen anyone who might be leaving the notes. I answer them all, including telling him that I somehow misplaced my keys and that my thesis adviser returned them this morning.

"But that was just today, right? That was after all this started?" he asks.

I nod. "Sorry, I thought you wanted to know every detail."

He holds up a hand. "I do. I wasn't being critical. Just trying to put together an accurate timeline. If your keys were lost before the notes started, that would lead me in a different direction than if you'd lost them after. No worries." Then he starts to go deeper. "Let's start with the first note," he says, nodding at it. He's left each one open so we can go over the contents while making minimal contact with each one. "When you read it, what did your gut tell you? Did you have any clue who would send it?"

I look over the words scrawled on the papers and read them again one by one.

"This is your fault."

"You've ruined everything."

"You thought I'd never find out what you did."

"You owe me."

I sit back in the chair and sigh. "I have no idea what any of these mean. When I got the first one, I'd sort of hoped it was some kind of mistake. But my name is on the outside of every note. Whoever left them meant the messages for me."

I watch as Josh scribbles on his notepad, and I notice for the first time he has the most colorful tattoos along his right forearm. I'm staring at the ink, trying to make out the designs, when he taps a long finger against the desk.

"It's obvious whoever sent these thinks you've taken something that this writer believes you're not entitled to." He squints at me and shakes his head. "Did you steal somebody's boyfriend or girlfriend? Could someone be pissed that you took their spot in the grad program?"

"No boyfriend or girlfriend," I say, hugging my arms close to my chest. I suddenly feel the chill from the window air conditioning unit, and I'm so, so cold. "I'm single. Haven't even dated anyone in over a year." It seems like a relevant bit of information, but I feel like the PI swallows a little bit loudly when I share that. "And it occurred to me that maybe somebody did have some grudge against me for getting into the program late, but who? I mean, if someone wanted a spot but didn't get into the program, how would they even be on campus to leave me notes?"

Josh shrugs. "Maybe it's someone who works on campus? Wasn't good enough to get in?"

"I don't know. I mean, it could be anyone talking about anything. It could be someone pissed I stole a parking spot, for all I know. I mean…" I drop my face into my hands and sigh. "That's why I hardly took them that seriously. I mean, I did. They're creepy and stalkerish, but I figured it could be a pointless prank or mistaken identity. Anything. Until the last one."

He nods. "That's the one that's got me worried. The writer is clearly escalating." He's quiet for a moment, and he taps the end of his pen against his full lips. "They didn't ask for anything from you until now. I wonder why…"

He looks me in the eye then, and my tummy does a little flip. I wonder what kind of people he works with every day. He can look scary, tough, and aggressive when he gets that interrogational look on his face. I wouldn't want to be on the receiving end of his pointed questions.

"Annie, you said your father's not made of money. What about you? Your mom? This person seems to think you have something that you're not entitled to. Can you think of anything they might be after?"

I meet his gaze, but my shoulders sink. "My mom passed away when I was six. Cancer."

"I'm so sorry," he says, filling the momentary silence between us.

I manage a half smile. "Thank you. It was a long time ago, but it never really stops hurting, you know? Mom was misdiagnosed. She had been complaining of stomach pains for a couple of days. She went to the doctor and got checked out, even went to the ER. The doctors took a scan, but they said she probably had a ruptured ovarian cyst that would heal. They told her to stay in bed for a few days, get some rest, and check back with them in two weeks if the pain didn't improve."

"Can you share any more?" Josh's voice is gentle. I can only imagine how much tragic and painful information he's had to pull out of people in this exact chair. Well, maybe in the chair in his office, but still. I look up at him and there's a softness in his eyes. He looks like he's hurting with me. That compassion gives me strength.

"Yeah," I say, meeting his crystal blue eyes. "She had a ruptured cyst but not the common kind they thought. It was a rare endometriotic tumor. A tumor on her ovary had ruptured. By the time Dad realized how sick she was, she had developed sepsis, and we lost her."

The room is quiet, only the gentle whirr of the motor on the window unit between us. I can feel the strong, cold air blowing the loose hairs across my neck and face.

"Annie, I'm sorry to ask, but was there a lawsuit?" Josh is looking at me, the pen he's holding gripped in a tight hand. Somehow, I feel like he's angry for me, and that makes me feel even more trusting toward him.

None of the other PIs I talked to spent more than five minutes with me before telling me their rates. I don't think Josh is asking about a lawsuit because he's only interested in whether I have money.

I shake my head. "My dad requested a second opinion from some other doctor, and he did talk to a lawyer after the funeral, but everyone told us it was a rare but unfortunate error. Not really a misdiagnosis. Just…" I shrug. "Weird shit happens to our bodies sometimes. There was no failure on the part of the doctors, no failure to provide a standard of care. Every doctor Dad talked to told him that if Mom had just complained or gone back… But she'd lain in bed and tried to tough it out. Without her going back, there was no way that anyone could have known how bad it was until it was too late. Not that it was her fault, of course. But no. There was no lawsuit. It was just a horrible tragedy that left my dad a single dad and me…"

"Motherless," Josh fills in.

I look up at him and am surprised at the warmth and understanding in his face. "Yeah," I say. "Motherless. After a couple of years of grieving, Dad went to law school at night. I think he wanted to go into personal injury or litigation or something, but he ended up with a really boring, stable job. He does real estate closings. He earns a decent living, but we're nothing special. We don't have anything more than the average person. Regular house, regular cars. No secret stash of money in a trust fund."

That leads me back to the whole reason I'm here. I literally can't imagine who would think I took anything away from them.

"I'm totally at a loss about what these notes mean."

Josh gets up from the desk and starts pacing the length of the office. His black jeans make little swishing sounds, his thick thighs moving with the perfectly molded fabric. That denim has been well broken-in, revealing a strong body underneath the professional demeanor.

"Well, somebody thinks you do. They may have been working up their courage with the first few notes. Maybe testing you out to see if you'd go to the police or campus security." He stops in his tracks and faces me. "Annie," he says, his deep voice skating along my nerve endings. I could fall into a seductive trance listening to that voice if I didn't have stomach-twisting worries on my mind at the moment. "I need to ask you something, and I need you to be completely honest with me."

I square my shoulders and nod. "What is it?"

He sighs and scrubs a hand through the long layers of his hair. "This may seem like I'm being insensitive, but I'm looking for motive. If you didn't take a position from someone, if you don't think it's related to money in some way, and you say you're single—" he squints at me, as if he can read the truth of my heart with one stare "—do you have any deep, dark secrets? Shit even your father doesn't know about?"

"I mean… Maybe?" I nervously pick at what's left of the polish covering my left thumb. "If there's anything, there's just one," I admit. "But I'm sure it has nothing to do with this. Seriously nothing."

He crosses his arms and arches a brow at me. The muscles in his beautifully inked biceps tighten, and he shakes his head. "I can't help you if I don't know all the facts. The whole truth," he demands. "I need to know everything about you, Annie. Even the things you're afraid to admit to yourself."

I sink back in the chair. I'm not proud of what I have to tell him, but it happened. And I suppose, no matter how irrelevant it is to what's going on with these notes, it can't hurt to tell him. "You have to promise you'll never tell my father," I say, biting my lower lip. "Dad doesn't know. And I don't want him to, okay?"

Josh gives me a look like I've asked him to pinkie swear to something, but he eventually nods. "I'll keep everything you tell me in confidence," he says. "Unless

I think it might compromise your safety, Annie. Then, all bets are off."

I nod, relieved because there's no way this secret has anything to do with these notes. This secret, as embarrassing and weird as it may be, will stay between us, I'm sure.

"It's not a big deal in the grand scheme," I admit. "But after I found out I was going to grad school, Dad threw a little office party for me. A going-away thing with cake and pizza. You know, no big deal. My dad's bookkeeper came, the new receptionist who they hired to replace me, and his law partner."

When I say law partner, it's like something in Josh's body language changes. He narrows his eyes and nods. "Did someone do something, Annie? Something inappropriate?"

I shake my head so abruptly that my braid flies onto my shoulder.

Josh looks like a pot about to boil over. I imagine in his line of work he sees the worst in people, but this isn't like that. It's just a little awkward.

"So, what happened?" Josh presses.

I nod. "After the little office party, Mr. Engler cornered me at my desk and asked me if he could take me to dinner. I wasn't sure how he meant it, like, as a date or something. He's my dad's partner and was my boss. He was always kind, and nothing ever felt weird until that moment. I said yes, but…"

All of a sudden, I feel super embarrassed admitting this to the strangely hot PI guy.

"I ghosted him. Didn't show. Didn't text. Nothing. I just couldn't. It felt too weird."

To my surprise, Josh looks really relieved. "So, what then? Did he start harassing you or anything?"

I shake my head. "He never said a thing about it. He never called me that night, didn't text me. He sent me an email a day or two after I blew him off."

"What did that email say?" Josh asks. "Do you still have it?"

I nod. "He said if I ever change my mind about grad school, he'd happily talk to my dad about giving me a bump in pay to stay at the law firm. He said I've been a bright spot and an exceptional employee, and he would love to see me pursue my dreams, but a practical career in the law would always be waiting for me."

Josh is quiet, but his shoulders seem to relax a bit. "Okay," he muses, squinting a little as he thinks. "So, no bad feelings with Dad's law partner. Do you think that dinner was supposed to be a date in his mind? Is there a chance he wanted to take you to dinner to ask you to stay at the firm?"

"I don't know." I sigh. "Maybe I should have gone to the dinner after all. Then I would know either way and I wouldn't feel like I did something wrong."

He drops his pen and shakes his head. "You did nothing wrong," he says forcefully. "Listen, Annie. I've seen people do a lot of shit to one another. Nasty, horrible, dangerous shit. Even to people they've known forever. Even to people they love. Always listen to your gut, and never, ever apologize for trusting your instincts."

"How can you do it?" I ask quietly. "With every-thing you see in people every day, how can you ever trust anyone?"

Josh rakes a hand through his hair, but then he meets my eyes when he answers. "You have to," he tells me. "Sometimes you get hurt. People will let you down. But if you never give people a chance and let them in, life is incredibly lonely."

I wonder if he's telling me this because he has been lonely. I could see the other PI's that I met with today being that way. Hardened, closed off to love and even friendship. I don't want that in my life. I don't want to be afraid to walk into my studio for fear of what some-body might want to do to me.

I lean forward on the desk and clasp my hands in front of me. "Whatever this is," I say, "can you help me, Josh? I don't have a ton of money, but I was thinking maybe if I hired you for security services, you could walk me to and from my studio for a few days. Maybe seeing someone—" I look his large, muscular frame up and down "—like you around will discourage whoever this is from bothering me."

Josh is quiet for a moment, tapping the end of the pen against his lips. "Security?" he asks. "You want to hire me like a bodyguard?"

I nod. "When I heard what the other PI's charge, I knew I probably couldn't afford a whole investigation. I'm not sure it even matters what this is about, as long as it stops. I Googled private security, and your listing came up. I thought I'd look into that as an option."

Something in Josh's shoulders shifts when I bring

up his rates. "Yeah," he sighs. "Most of us take a retainer to start. We add on expenses, if there are any. Mileage or gas, stuff like that."

He asks a few questions, like where I go to school, and he calculates the distance between his office and campus. Then he asks about my budget and whether my father knows anything about what's going on.

"I really don't want to go to my father," I admit. "He's paying for school, which is a huge, huge gift. If he finds out anything weird is going on, he'll pull me out, and all that tuition will go to waste."

"Annie…" Josh shakes his head. "If this escalates, for your own safety, you may need to go to your father. Hell, you may need to go to the police. I recommend you go now, just to get a report on file. There hasn't been a demand for money or any other coercion yet, so there's not much the cops can do. It's not clear if you're being stalked, if someone's trying to extort money from you…"

The more he talks, the more a sense of uncomfortable foreboding settles over my entire body like a heavy blanket.

I stand from the chair and pace the lobby, the heavy panic deciding to settle in my chest. I've got to move, got to shake these feelings off before they sink me. "Who the heck would stalk me? I barely know anyone on campus yet. I mean, I hardly have any friends. How could I have enemies?"

Josh stands too, and while he doesn't approach me, he does look me straight in the eye. "Annie, you're beautiful. You never know who might notice you and get weird-ass ideas in their head. Stalking doesn't have to be about someone knowing you. It could be anyone who *thinks* they know you or someone who *wants* to know you." He crosses his arms over his chest and looks at me harshly. "I'll take your case," he says abruptly, then turns and walks into his office.

"Wait...what?" We haven't even talked about money or how I'm going to pay him.

He returns a moment later with his laptop. "I'm going to take some basic personal information," he tells me, opening the lid and tapping the keys. "I won't charge a retainer, and I'll work by the hour. Can you afford this?"

He turns the screen to face outward, so I go back to the desk and bend over to read the client service agreement. I scan the fields he's filled in, and my mouth drops open when I see his hourly rate.

"Is that what you charge?" I ask. "That can't be right."

He points a long finger farther down the page to another paragraph. "I'm going to limit my initial investigation to ten hours. If I can't get your answers in that amount of time, we'll revisit this rate. Fair?"

I can't believe what I'm seeing. I gave up my apartment to move in to the much cheaper dorms. I paid my room and board out of my savings, and now that I'm not working at all, what's left in my account has to cover everything. I was only a receptionist when I worked for my dad, so it's not like I was making big bucks and was able to save up a ton of cash. But the rate Josh is charging me is something I can easily afford. But it's far too little, in my opinion. And I'm not sure why he's cut me a deal like this. Unless…

No. He's not given me any creepy vibes at all. He's been nothing but warm and professional. And still, I have to ask the question.

"Why?" I search the contours of his face for answers. For secrets. Is he a wolf in sheep's clothing and I'm about to open the door and let him in? "Why would you do this for me?"

He sniffs and then waves at me as if to dismiss the question. "I'm between corporate gigs," he says simply. "I have some extra time at the moment. I'd rather take a pay cut and have some work to tide me over. But there are a few conditions you'll have to follow."

Here it comes. The strings attached to his too-good-to-be-true offer. I haven't signed anything yet. I am, after all, the daughter of a lawyer. Now it's my turn to cross my arms and consider his conditions.

"What are they?" I ask, looking over at the notes spread on his desk. If I don't like what he says, I'll take the notes and my backpack and just leave. It's that simple. I may be in some kind of danger, but I'm not powerless.

"You tell me everything that happens as it happens," he says. "Nothing is too big or too small. You take this seriously, Annie. What I mean is, don't tolerate anything. Don't sit there and take it, Annie. You deserve to feel safe on campus, out in the world. You speak up. No matter what it is, you tell me. If I'm not there, you yell. You tell somebody to fuck off if they even look at you funny. You hear me? You deserve better than this bullshit, and we're going to get to the bottom of it. But I can't put a stop to it if I don't know what's hurting you. Are we clear?"

Tears sting my eyes, and I nod.

Josh may look like a big, bad wolf, but I have a feeling I may have just met my knight in shining armor.

CHAPTER 4
ARROW

"COME ON," I say, closing the lid to my laptop. Annie's signed my standard client service agreement, so it's time to get to work.

"Come on?" She stands and slings the backpack over her tanned shoulder, after putting the folder of letters back inside. "Where are we going?"

I slip my phone into my pocket and grab the keys to my truck. "Campus." I already have a plan in mind. I need to get the lay of the land first—where she lives and works. Maybe then I can figure out how this person is getting the letters to her. If I can figure out how, I'm one step closer to figuring out who. In the meantime, there's more digging I plan to do to get as close as I can to the why. "I want to see everything. Your studio, your dorm room. All of it."

"Umm…" She looks uncomfortable, like she's having second thoughts, but then nods. "Yeah, that's a good idea. Should we ride together? We can take my car. I have a fully paid student parking pass."

I stifle a groan. The last thing I want is to be chauffeured around, but if she drives, I'll have a better opportunity to pay attention to the surroundings without focusing on the road.

"Yeah," I say. "That's probably a good idea."

She giggles, and I realize I echoed almost exactly what she just said. I crack a grin. She's cute. No, she's gorgeous. And sweet. There's no way I'm going to let some shady bastard scare her—or worse.

After I lock up the office, I get serious. I turn to follow her to the car but nearly stop when the bright sunshine hits her perfect smile. She looks relaxed and light. The tension and awkwardness from inside evaporate like a drop of water in the Florida heat.

Something inside me stirs hard, and I have to look away to stop from thinking of her as more than just a client. More than a woman who has a credible threat to her safety. She's hired me, and I clench my hands into fists, reminding myself to keep a professional distance.

She almost bounces on her flip-flops as she leads me to a silver Honda sedan. "You don't look like the kind of guy who'd ever let a woman drive him around."

"I'm normally not," I grunt. And yet here I am, stalking up to the passenger side of a modest, but well-kept four-door sedan.

While she's given me no reason to distrust her, I'm relieved that the car she drives fits with the story she's told. So many of my clients have the kind of disposable income most of us only dream of. I've tailed wives, daughters, and lovers in cars that cost more than my condo.

Annie Hancock isn't a flashy, spoiled lawyer's daughter.

Which makes the last letter she received all the more curious. Who could want her to pay? Pay for what? With what? I'm going to have to take pics of those letters now that I've taken her case, so we have a record if she does, in fact, have to turn them over to the police.

She unlocks the doors and climbs behind the wheel.

As I get inside, I notice bags lining the footwell in the back seat. "Anything valuable in there?" I slide into the passenger seat and fasten the seat belt.

Annie frowns, a little crinkle forming between her brows. A fucking adorable crinkle. I shove the thought away and watch as she lowers a pair of sunglasses over her eyes and starts the car.

"No. Why?" she asks. "Just thrift store finds. I upcycle and recycle materials as much as I can."

"Trunk might be safer. Doesn't take much to tempt a smash-and-grab with the bags left in plain sight." I realize I'm staring at her when I see the frown that tugs at her full lips replaced by a playful smile.

"The trunk might be safer, but…"

"Annie," I say, trying to adjust my legs to fit in the small car. "If there's a body back there, I'm not sure I want to know."

She laughs but then quickly sobers. She adjusts the rearview mirror and backs out of the spot. "I probably shouldn't laugh," she says. "I wish all of this were just a joke."

"You don't know what this is," I say, trying to sound

reassuring. "And you don't have to. That's my job now. I'm going to get answers."

On the short drive to the Florida Arts campus, I drill her about her routine. She answers every question until I bring up the uncomfortable stuff.

"So, I know you said earlier there were no exes," I say, trying to word this in a way that won't freak her out. "Nobody out there who thinks you stole her husband?"

Annie flicks a quick look at me, her long braid dusting her shoulders. I can't see her eyes behind the sunglasses, but she shakes her head and draws that full lower lip between her teeth.

"No," she says. "There's nothing like that." She hesitates a minute, so I wait.

I've learned that the full truth very rarely comes out on the first try. I get the feeling that Annie's smart, so I don't try to trap her with the tricks that would work on my usual clients, repeating the question in different ways or "accidentally" misremembering what they said, forcing the person to clarify what they meant the first time. I can't tell you how many times a new truth comes out when someone thinks that you won't remember what they originally said.

What she says next, though, surprises me.

"I... This may sound weird, but...I can really only think of one person who might have a grudge against me. But I can't..." She shrugs. "I mean, you probably see the worst in people. I'm sure nothing surprises you."

I nod but stay quiet. I knew there was more coming. There always is.

She starts to talk just as we pull onto campus. I split my attention between what she's saying and noticing every single thing I'm seeing around me. Even worse is what I'm not seeing.

First, there's no security barring the public from entering campus. Any vehicle can drive past the massive stucco-and-metal sculpture that is about the only thing separating the palm-tree-lined streets of the neighborhood from the campus property. No security station. No signs proclaiming this is private property. Nada.

Fuck.

Annie turns into a parking structure right off Arts Lane. This, too, is open to the public. There are no automated arms, no key fobs. Literally nothing to stop any dickhead from following her in. She drives into the structure, parks in an unnumbered spot, which means no assigned parking, and pulls a hangtag from a pocket in the driver's side door.

"Thank God," I say quietly.

"What?" she asks, hanging the plastic bar code from her mirror.

"At least you don't drive around with that thing hanging in your car. Anybody anywhere you park can see that you're a student. Those fucking hangtags should be illegal. They are the least secure form of parking enforcement out there. Especially for students."

She looks serious. "Not secure but cheap, I bet. I'm all for whatever it takes to keep my costs down, but when you look at it that way…" She frowns and turns a little in her seat to face me. "How do you do it?" she asks. "How do you see the worst in everything and not feel angry all the time? I don't know. Maybe you are angry." She huffs a sigh and leans back in her seat. As the engine goes quiet, the car falls silent. Her question hangs heavy between us.

"I do get angry, but not the way you might think," I say, wanting for some reason I can't fully understand to give her the truth. "I don't walk through the world seeing every possible hazard, every worst-case scenario, or else it would be hard to get out of bed in the morning."

She's watching me talk, sucking her lower lip between her teeth.

"But there are times when my experience with, well, with the worst that people can do qualifies me to make sure those people do as little harm to others as possible. That's what keeps me going."

She searches my face. "So, you do this to help people? Why not become a police officer or something? Did you ever want to do that?"

I laugh at that. "There's no way anybody's letting me enforce the laws. I don't have a squeaky-clean past, and I've spent a lot of time hanging with sinners not saints. I think I'm right where I need to be. Catching cheats, liars, and stopping crimes when I can, before they happen."

"I never thought about it that way." She leans toward me and reaches into the back seat to grab her backpack.

She can't quite reach it, and her face is just inches from my shoulder. She blushes, a crimson cloud blooming across her chest. "I'll grab that when we get out."

We unbuckle our belts and step out into the heat of the parking garage. While she gets her backpack, I look around, checking for exits, security cameras, security phones. I don't like what I'm seeing. Rather, what I'm not seeing.

"You were saying earlier, Annie," I remind her as she locks her car. "About somebody who might have a grudge."

I want her talking, but at the same time, I'm in threat-assessment mode. I can already tell that whoever is leaving these notes for Annie doesn't have to try very hard to gain access to the campus itself. I can only hope that the rest of campus is more secure.

It's hard to believe a private college campus has nothing in the way of functional security.

"Oh yeah." She adjusts the backpack over her shoulders and points left. She follows a sidewalk that is artfully decorated with words stamped into the concrete. I squint through the dark filter of my sunglasses to make out the details.

"Jesus Christ," I grumble, stopping and glaring down at the sidewalk. Some of the letters are worn a bit by foot traffic, but most of the words etched into the path are dark and stand out in sharp relief to the light concrete. "Dream. Rest. Balance," I read. I shake my head and scoff. "Let me guess. All these little pretty phrases lead to the dorms."

I feel Annie stiffen beside me, and I immediately regret my choice of words.

"Fuck," I sigh, scrubbing a hand through my hair. "I'm sorry." I jab a finger toward the sidewalk. "This is a goddamn security nightmare."

I step close to her and lower my voice.

"Do you realize that this is literally a glowing neon sign pointing to where you live and sleep?" I turn and whip around, gesturing toward the street, the parking structure, all of it. "This place is as easy to access as the goddamn supermarket and easier to navigate than a preschool. A bad guy wouldn't have to try very hard to do a lot of damage here."

She looks like she's either going to curse me out or start crying, but she surprises me by placing a hand on my arm and squeezing. "You're right," she says in a choked voice.

Her skin on mine is warm, and even though she's only gripping my forearm… Fuck. She's soft. Strong. It takes everything in me to keep my eyes from her long, toned legs as she rocks close to me.

"I'm so grateful you're doing this," she says. "None of this stuff is anything I would ever notice. Not until now. You're totally right. But now, it's too late." She looks down at her hand and releases my arm. "Sorry," she murmurs, but something in her voice makes my cock take notice. I think she's apologizing for touching me, not what she said.

But I'm not sorry. Not even a little.

I'm not normally attracted to clients, but then again, I've never had a client like Annie before. Hot, horny housewives are easy to keep at arm's length. But this assignment is going to test my professional boundaries in a way that makes me very fucking happy I only signed on for ten hours of work.

Ten hours of blue balls is more than any man should have to take. And the very last thing this woman needs is to feel any kind of vibe off me.

I'm safe.

Here to protect her. Not to get close to her. No matter that the way she's looking at me melts my guts into a puddle.

"Should we keep going?" I ask.

She nods, but she pulls her eyes from mine a little too slowly. I'm cursing the heat of the afternoon and the heat from her that I feel in every inch of my body. I rub my eyes under my sunglasses and follow her along the sidewalk to a nondescript building. A small sign out front announces it as the Laura Woodward Residence Center. I glare at the building, only somewhat relieved to find a warning posted on the front door.

Notice: This property is protected by electronic surveillance.

The sticker affixed to the upper corner of the glass door is so faded by the sun, it's hardly readable. But the icon of the video camera is unmistakable. I'm praying the sign isn't for show. There's got to be an eye in the sky someplace actually recording the premises.

I nod without pointing to the sign. "Where's the camera?"

She widens her eyes. "What do you mean?"

I lift my brows and look up at the sign. "Security surveillance. There's got to be one somewhere."

"A camera? I don't know," she says, pushing the sunglasses onto her forehead. "I've never noticed. Honestly, I've never even looked at that sign before now." She looks discouraged and tugs the sunglasses from her face. "How the hell have I never noticed this stuff before?"

"Most people don't," I reassure her.

My stomach knots, but I'm not surprised. Half these signs are old. Left up because just the idea that there are security cameras is often enough of a deterrent to make the bad guys think twice.

I've had plenty of clients keep signs in their windows long after the security system broke, went down, or simply stopped being paid for.

A sign does not mean there is surveillance. I can only hope a private school like this would do better, but my expectations are pretty fucking low at this point.

"Come on," I say, totally not surprised when I'm able to open the front door. No locks. No passcode. No keycards. Fucking great. "Tell me about this grudge."

I hold the exterior door open for Annie and keep my eyes as far away from her ass as I'm humanly able to manage as she walks past me.

"My dad's girlfriend," she explains. "Dad was seeing Cathy for a year or so. It was pretty casual at first, but I don't really know what happened. Dad said she started getting serious. Wanted to move in together, but I guess he wasn't ready for that, or so he said at the time." Annie's flip-flops echo against the tile floor as she leads me toward an elevator. "Don't get me wrong. Cathy and I got along fine. I wasn't a huge fan of hers, but there was no tension. No problems to speak of. Dad seemed happy enough to have someone, but it wasn't this, like, love story. You know? I mean, if my dad had really wanted her to move in, I would have supported it."

"Would you really?" I press, watching as she pushes the button for the elevator. "First comes living together, and then, not long after, most women would expect a ring."

She frowns slightly. "I mean…yeah. I think that's what Cathy wanted. After she and Dad broke up, she sent me a kind of shitty text."

I perk up at that. "What did she say?"

Annie presses the number seven. There are eight floors in this building. I make a note to ride up to the top before I leave to check out roof access and anything else that might help me do my job.

"The text was weird," she admits, settling her back against the wall of the elevator. She looks me up and down, her eyes thoughtful. "She said, I hope you get what you want, Annie. He's all yours now."

"That sounds ominous," I mutter. "Not to mention fucking weird. She meant your dad?"

She shrugs, and the elevator dings to announce we're at the seventh floor. "I guess. Maybe my dad used me as an excuse to break it off? I don't know. He's been going through a lot the last year, and every time I brought it up, he was too tired to deal."

Once we're off the elevator, I scan the hallway. The

elevator is at the end of the hallway that leads right to student rooms. I can see decorated doors, some open with students walking or talking across the hall, and a few people out in the halls. The place is decidedly tame for a dorm full of artists.

"Classes are in session right now," Annie says, pointing to an old-fashioned clock on the wall. "There are usually more people around than this. Undergrads are on floors one through six, but seven and eight are grad students, so it's normally a lot more boring up here."

"Great," I say, meaning it. More people around meant fewer chances that a stranger could come and go unnoticed. That is, if Annie's letter-writer is, in fact, a stranger. If it's someone who belongs here, who blends in, that just makes the whole situation that much harder to assess.

"So," I say as we walk down the hall toward her room. "What's the guest policy in the dorms? Is anyone going to check my identification? Will anyone even know I'm here?"

Annie shakes her head. "There is a policy of no non-students staying overnight," she says. She chuckles and rolls her eyes. "But I can tell you that's really not enforced. The exterior doors are locked at ten. After that, there is a security guard posted out front. We have to take food deliveries out there, and no guests are allowed in. Other buildings have keycard access after they close, but I guess they had too many incidents with drunk kids losing their keycards."

I'm about to say I'm relieved there is a security

guard someplace on this so-called campus, but Annie has stopped in front of a door and is jiggling her key in the lock.

"That's weird," she says softly.

"What?" I demand, stepping close to her. "What is it?"

"I turned the key, and I think I just locked the door. Like it was maybe unlocked."

"Do you remember locking it? Do you ever leave the door unlocked?" I ask. Annie's door is nondescript. Just a basic metal plate with the room number etched into it. No colorful decorations or her name signifying who lives there. I'm relieved for that much, at least.

"I always lock it, but I did lose my keys for a while this morning." She turns to face me, her eyes wide. "Shit, Josh…"

Her hand is on the knob, and she's turning it, looking back at me as though I can stop whatever scary thing might be ahead.

"Annie, wait," I say, but it's too late. She pushes the door open, and we see what's happened to her room at exactly the same time.

"Oh my God…" She stops in her tracks just as I start to move forward. Her backpack hits me in the chest, and she spins on a heel. "I'm sorry," she blurts, but I don't move.

The next thing I know, her face is buried in my chest.

CHAPTER 5
ANNIE

THEY'VE BEEN in my room.

And they've fucking trashed it.

Any hope I had that this was a harmless prank fades away along with the last shreds of my courage. Maybe this isn't the work of the same person sending me those notes. But something in my gut tells me that it is all related.

It has to be. Just has to be.

The reality hits me like a ton of bricks the moment I see everything I own wrecked.

The sour taste of sickness rises in my throat. This can't be happening. I don't believe it. But it's real. Even though the proof is right in front of my eyes.

I have to face this. Whatever this is. But at least I took the first step in hiring Josh.

But I can't stop myself from closing my eyes and turning around, ready to run. "Shit. I'm sorry, I'm sorry." As soon as my face hits the smooth, hard muscles of Josh's chest, I realize what I've done. If I weren't scared half out of my damn mind, I'd have wanted to spend a lot more time chest-to-chest with him.

Inappropriate, yes, but I can't help it.

I would be back in my car driving the hell out of here already, but there's a massive, tattooed wall standing between me and escape. My personal body-guard-slash-PI is sweet, smart, and freaking sexy. But he's also big. There's no way I'm getting around him and running away until he lets me go.

"It's all right. Just stay behind me." His voice is a growl as he pushes me to his back.

I'm just relieved he seems totally unfazed by the fact that I practically launched myself into his arms. I don't have time to be embarrassed.

I move out of the way and stand in the hallway as Josh shoves the door all the way open. I can't very well run off while he walks headfirst into this, so I stand there, knees shaking and sweat breaking out on my forehead.

"Bathroom?" he whispers.

I nod and point to a closed door. When I first moved in, I was relieved that the rooms on the grad student floors had private bathrooms. Only the undergrads share showers and toilets. But now, all my excitement at the luxury fades to misery.

Someone could still be in my room.

But that doesn't stop Josh.

"Wait here." He walks softly into my room, stepping around the chaos that has unfolded in front of us.

My eyes sting with tears as I look at what's been done.

Whoever did this, they ruined everything.

The mattress has been pulled off the bed. It hangs over the edge of the frame, sagging in defeat. My pillows have been shredded, even the pink faux-fur throw pillows that I hand-made. Clumps of pink fur have settled in piles of downy feathers.

It's more than just a mess. It feels like a message.

The insides of everything I've loved are just gutted.

My closet door is open, and every top, skirt, and pair of pants has been pulled from the hangers and tossed on the floor. Every drawer hangs open like gaping mouths, my underwear, socks, and tanks scattered like confetti.

The books have not been tossed from my shelves, but I suspect that's because that would have made too much noise. The books that I had on the built-in desk have pages torn out and crumpled.

The few posters, mostly inexpensive art prints I'd hung on the walls, have not just been torn down but ripped in half.

And all my art supplies—yarn, fabric, buttons—were dumped into a pile. It could take me days to sort through this mess. And even then, I might not be able to salvage anything.

Everything I own has been touched by some stranger. Someone who took the time to come into my private space and terrorize me.

My heart starts to thunder, and my knees go weak. I

want to look behind me, make sure there's no one there in the hallway, but Josh is saying my name.

"Annie? Come on." His voice is steady, and he extends a hand to me. "Bathroom's clear. It's safe."

I look at his tattooed forearm, the long fingers that beckon me to join him. I'm stuck in a fear spiral, not sure whether to run into my room, toward all the things that make my life mine, or run away.

Instead, I stay rooted in place.

I think I might be in shock.

Nothing like this has ever happened to me before. I've never even seen a car accident. I don't have any clue what the right thing to do is.

I shake my head as fear and the very beginnings of anger start to burn in my belly. "I can't," I say, squinting. "I can't…"

"Annie." Josh has crossed the floor, stepping as carefully as he can around the piles of my belongings.

I try not to notice the bras and boy briefs lying right there in the open for anyone to see. I swallow back a sob.

"Annie." Josh is close now. He offers me his tattoo-covered hand. "I need you to come inside, please. We need to see if anything was taken or if the place was just torn up. You're safe with me. I'm not going to let anything happen to you. I promise."

I look down at the hand he's holding out to me again, willing myself to accept his help. To trust him. My palms break out in an immediate sweat, but I take his tattooed hand. I take one step inside the room, and Josh reaches past me to close the door. I sway a little bit on my feet, and the next thing I know, his hands are around my arms.

Holding me up. Supporting me.

"Hey," he says, dipping his chin to look into my eyes. "Hey, hey, Annie. Look at me, okay? Stay with me."

I give him a weak smile and look into his deep blue eyes. "I'm not going to faint," I tell him. "At least, I don't think so."

"Good," he says, his voice reassuring and smooth. He sounds relieved, but there's something in his tone that's encouraging in a way that makes the tiny hairs on my arms stand up. "That's good, Annie."

The praise in his voice makes me feel a confusing mix of reactions. It's completely the wrong time and totally the wrong place to feel anything for my bodyguard, but the way he croons at me, it's hard not to imagine him calling me a good girl in a very, very different situation.

I nod, trying to brush away the traitorous thoughts about Josh. "So, what…what do I do? I mean, it's all ruined. Everything I own."

His face looks grim, and a shadow passes over his handsome face. "Fuck, Annie. I'm sorry. Can you look through what's here? Can you tell if anything is missing? Just don't move or touch anything. We're going to need to call the police in a minute. They'll want to know if anything was stolen or if this is something else."

I should have known that's what he'd say. And I know it's stupid, but the thought of calling the police is the thing that makes all of this real. I drop my backpack and cover my face with my hands just as the tears start to fall.

"Tell me it's a coincidence." I wipe the tears from my face, but I don't know how I'm going to pull it together. Where to go from here? I mean, my God. I can't sleep here tonight. But I also can't go to my father's.

My thoughts must be plainly readable on my face because Josh is close to me again, his hands on my arms. "Hey," he says. "One step at a time. One minute at a time. You got this."

But I don't got this. I literally don't have anything. Not anymore. And definitely not the feeling of safety I used to have.

I stand there quietly, absorbing the calming strength that his touch brings. I'm grateful for it. I need it. Even if it makes me feel weak to need it. Isn't this exactly what I hired him for, though?

It's okay, I tell myself. He's doing his job. He probably hugs weeping women every day. This is just that. Nothing more.

I take a few steady breaths when a sharp knock at the door has me leaping out of my flip-flops and straight at Josh.

"What the fuck," I blurt out. My heart starts rattling in my chest in time with my irrational thoughts.

They're back. Whoever did this is here. They're back. I know then that I don't have what it takes to be a fighter. In a fight-or-flight situation, I'm more likely to grow wings and freaking fly than open that door and fight back. I hate that about myself. It's not the kind of thing anyone wants to believe, but it becomes clear what kind of man Josh is when he laces his fingers through mine and tugs me so I'm standing behind him.

"Who's there?" he barks.

"Who the hell is in there? Annie Hannie? You okay?"

I place a hand on Josh's back as relief washes over me for a moment. "It's my RA," I tell him, my voice shaking. "Resident adviser. She supervises the floor. She's like a peer counselor."

"You want her here?" he whispers. "I can tell her to bug off."

"No, let her in. She's going to have to find out about this anyway." I squeeze his hand and then release him, immediately missing the comforting heat from his touch.

He nods once and turns the knob, opening the door to Neveah.

"Who the hell might you be?" She's glaring at him, and I can see her trying to peer around him to look for me. "Annie?" she calls out. "Hey, babe, you okay?"

I peek around Josh and see Neveah's Mama Bear grimace. This has got to look bad. A man she's never seen or heard of before hiding me behind him and my room looking like something out of a horror film— minus the blood. My stomach does a gnarly flip just thinking about blood and what might have happened if I'd been in my room when whoever did this was here.

I don't know if it's adrenaline or stress or me just being out of my mind at the moment, but I push myself forward and step under Josh's arm. He looks surprised for a second, but then he just goes with it. He curls an arm over my shoulders protectively and holds me close to his side.

"I'm right here," I tell her weakly. "And I'm fine." I smile up at Josh, whose eyes haven't left my RA's face. "Neveah, this is Josh."

I leave out any other details. She is eyeing him suspiciously, and I think the less I say, the better. I don't see any reason why Neveah shouldn't think that Josh is with me. He doesn't look that much older than me, and the last thing I want is for her to suspect I've been having trouble that I didn't let her in on.

"Josh, hmmm? Haven't heard anything about a Josh before. And this?" She motions wildly with her hand, her temper firing up with every passing second. "What in the goddamn holy hell is this? Did you trash this room?"

"Annie lost her keys for a time this morning. It looks like whoever found them decided to ransack her room before turning them in."

Neveah's mouth drops open. "Are you fucking kidding me? That's what this is?" She grows quiet for a minute and sounds a lot less accusatory. "I'm going to need to call campus security."

"Please do." Josh's voice is clear and calm. "And the local police. I'm not sure this is something campus police can handle."

Neveah crosses her arms over her chest. "You have a hell of a lot to say for a guy I didn't know existed until two minutes ago."

Josh tightens his hold on me. "Look, Neveah, is it? I'm

not here to cause any problems. Annie and I just walked in and found the place like this. I checked to make sure there was no one still in here. We had about a two-minute head start, or I would already have dialed the cops myself."

"Well, I work for the school," she blurts out, "and protocol is to call campus security first. They make the determination whether to involve local PD."

"I understand that." Josh's voice is patient, but I can tell by the slight tension in his hand against my skin that it's taking an effort. "But this is a matter for the police. This room was broken in to—unlawfully entered —and…"

He's gathering steam, and if I know Neveah, she'll meet his passion with her own. As much as I appreciate these two wanting to help, I want to get this over with and get the hell out of this room. I need to think. I need to clear my head.

Maybe because I'm not thinking right, I turn to Josh, chest-to-chest, and lean in to the lie that Josh and I are dating in a way I will probably regret later. I lift a hand to his cheek. "Hey," I say softly. "Neveah's a friend. Let's let her handle this the way she needs to. I don't want her getting into any kind of trouble because of this. Okay?"

I hope I'm blocking Neveah from seeing the look on my face and the blush I can feel storming across my cheeks and chest.

She's the only real friend I've made at this school so far. And I've even hidden everything from her because I was in denial that it was any big deal. I've been so, so wrong. About so many things. But still, I don't want her to get hurt in any way because of me.

Josh swallows, and I watch his throat bob up and down. Even his neck, sprinkled with bristles, is sexy.

"Okay?" I ask again, trailing my hand down the side of his face. I plead with him with my eyes—at least I hope I am, but I very well could be looking like an idiot.

Josh clears his throat and nods. "Yeah, right. Whatever she needs to do."

Neveah crosses her arms over her chest. "I'm going to my room to get my phone. I have to ask both of you to stay here so the campus police can talk to you." She turns to leave but then turns back and points at me, a sly half smile on her lips. "And you and I are going to have a talk later, girl. You've been holding out. And I thought we were friends."

She gives me a grin that lets me know she's forgiven me and then heads off down the hall for her phone.

As soon as we're alone, I turn to Josh. "I'm so, so sorry," I breathe. "That was so inappropriate, I just…I didn't want her thinking you'd kidnapped me or something."

Josh isn't smiling, but he doesn't look angry. He's looking lost in thought as if he's replaying something in his head. "What do you know about Neveah?" he asks. "How old is she?"

I shrug. "I assume around my age. Twenty-five or so. Why?"

He's quiet. "Nothing. How close are you two?"

"She's the only friend I've made here so far."

"All right, then. Here's our story," he says, leaning

close. "I'm twenty-nine, and we met just a few weeks before you came here. It started off casual at first, but you left for school and I want to get serious, but I am trying to respect your space here at art school. That work?"

"How did we meet?" I ask quietly.

"I think we should be honest about what I do," he says, but I can tell he's holding something back. "Try to avoid bringing it up if you can. Definitely don't mention that you hired me. Your dad does real estate law? Closings and stuff?"

"Yes, exactly."

"I bought a condo a year ago. Let's just say I met you when I hired your dad to handle the closing. Low-key on the details and timeline. If she asks, give her just enough that it sounds plausible. That work?"

"It's perfect, actually. You're brilliant." I can't believe he thinks so fast on his feet. I mean, I guess I'm the one who thought to give Neveah the impression that we are together, but he makes the story work.

I'm not sure whether to be worried that he can so easily lie or be impressed. He is smart, and I feel like he is really looking out for what is best for me. I feel good about this story even if I don't feel good about this entire situation.

"Give me your number," I tell him, pulling my cell phone from my backpack. "I need you in my contacts."

He tells me his number, and I quickly punch it in then send him a text so he has mine. I hear the buzz of the notification coming from his back pocket just as Neveah returns to my room.

"Babe," Josh says loud enough for her to overhear. "Pick up your backpack. You don't want anything in there to get mixed up with this mess."

I'm curious what he means by that… Is he trying to say something about the letters?

"Thanks, hon," I say, throwing in the endearment to play along. It feels weird rolling off my tongue, and I practically giggle. But then I think about the letters in my backpack and wonder what to do.

Should I mention them when campus security gets here? Then they're going to ask why I never reported them before. My stomach does another death spiral.

"Annie?" I feel Josh's eyes searching mine, and I meet his gaze. "When the officer gets here," he tells me slowly, "can you tell them if anything's missing?"

"I can try," I say.

My laptop should be in my studio. I only had books and the letters in my backpack. The only things of value in my room are my personal items. It's not like I'll be able to tell if a pair of underwear is missing. Not with everything like this.

When the campus police officer arrives, the whole thing is a lot less scary than I expect. The officer looks like he's about ready for the grave. He is unarmed but has a radio. He widens his eyes at the mess and asks me what happened. If we're both students. He takes our names and asks how long we've been dating. It's clear at first that he thinks there's been a fight between Josh and me and that one of us lost our temper and trashed my room.

"No, no," I say. "Nothing like that."

"Annie came to my office to meet for lunch," Josh says. "She decided she wanted to grab some supplies and work in my spare office for the afternoon." He looks at me with a look so sultry, I actually feel myself melt a little. "My fault," Josh continues, his lie so enticing I half want to believe it. "She's been spending so much time on campus, I wanted a little time with her. I was trying to convince her to get dinner and maybe stay off campus for the night. If you know what I mean, sir."

The officer writes down everything we're saying on a piece of paper and gives Josh a look at that last part, while my face burns at the mere suggestion that I'd spend the night with Josh. I hope Neveah thinks it's because I'm embarrassed to mention that to a strange, old guy—not because the idea is thrilling in the weirdest way.

The campus police officer is making notes, but he hardly comes inside the room. He inspects the door, and when he doesn't see any damage to it, he seems to make his mind up about what happened here since I explained how I lost my keys.

"Well, young lady, this is quite a mess to clean up. I'm going to guess somebody found your keys and decided to ransack the room while they had the chance." He narrows his eyes at me. "You got any drugs in here? Anything of value that someone might want?"

I shake my head. "No, nothing like drugs," I say. "Just my clothes and art supplies." I meet Josh's eyes, and he gives me an encouraging nod.

"Well, if nothing's missing, there's no cause to call

the local police," he says. "No theft, no crime. Looks like some mischief to me. Keep a better hold of your keys, Miss Hancock," he says. "College is an opportunity to have fun. But let's not forget not everyone is trustworthy."

I'm suddenly furious at this campus cop's reaction. Keep better hold of my keys? No crime here? What if I had never received any letters and something like this had happened? They'd tell me to be more responsible with my shit and walk away? That's it?

I open my mouth to say something, and I look to Josh. He doesn't give me any cues. Doesn't tell me to calm down. He looks as furious as I am, but he doesn't say anything. I take a hint from him and do the same, even though I'm surprised at my own sense of justice. Maybe I'm more of a fighter than I thought.

I don't want to believe that something this scary could happen and for it not to be taken seriously by the very people who are supposed to investigate.

The officer and Neveah talk quietly for a minute about filing an incident report and her getting him to sign off on it.

Josh stands beside me, his arms crossed over his chest. He's glaring, so I set a hand on his arm and he seems to soften. We're developing a weird little way of communicating without speaking. And while it feels intimate for someone I've only known a few hours, it also feels natural.

As if I've known him much, much longer. I can trust Josh, and even more than that, I want him by my side through this.

Before the officer leaves, Josh addresses him in a quiet and respectful voice.

"Sir? Are there, by any chance, any surveillance cameras in the building? Maybe there's a way to see who entered Annie's room. This may not be a police matter, but I would think it's an issue of public safety. Anyone willing to break in to a student's room like this —" He waves his tattoo-covered hand around the room. "It may be nothing more than criminal mischief and trespassing, but I think I'd feel better knowing who it was who did this."

"No cameras in the building," the guy says, narrowing his eyes at Josh. "Privacy issues. It was probably just some student looking for a laptop or some cash. I'm sorry you have to clean up this mess, Miss Hancock."

Then Neveah and the officer head out down the hall, leaving Josh and me alone.

"You did good," he says, and that same warmth floods my body at his praise. He shakes his head and looks pissed. "That cop-in-a-box clearly isn't taking this seriously. At least we know the camera situation now."

Josh looks down at the mess. "Can you grab some clothes and whatever supplies you need? You know you can't stay here tonight."

I'd already started thinking about that. The mess alone is going to take me days to clean. I have classes and projects to think about. And how the hell am I going to sleep here? I mean, forget the fact that my pillows have been gutted. *I'm* gutted by what this means. What would have happened if I'd lost my keys but come back to my room?

I have to think about what's next and what I need to do to be safe. I mentally calculate the balance in my bank account. I can't call my dad. I can't tell him about this. I can't go home right now.

"I need to get my laptop," I say. "You wanted to see my studio, right? Then, I'll take you back to your office and figure out what to do for the night."

Josh is quiet. "Do you want a minute? Need some privacy to pack?"

I see him staring at a sheer red bra, its underwire curving like a bloody grin. "What's the point," I mutter.

I know he's trying to be nice, and I should be more thankful. I should be more gracious. Right now, I'm defeated. I don't have the money, the means, the support to face this. I've already used up how many hours of Josh's time. That ten hours isn't going to get me answers. And now I need to spend money on a hotel I can't afford.

I don't know what I did to get into this situation, but the sooner Josh figures it out, the sooner I can get my life back on track.

If he can't, I won't be able to stay in school. I won't be able to get my degree and make the art that could change the course of my future. My dreams, like all of my belongings, will be wrecked. The thought of that brings the tears back to my eyes.

"Actually," I say, sniffling, "Would you mind? I'll just be a minute."

He studies my face, and again I get the sense that

there are things he's thinking that he's not saying. But he doesn't say anything and heads out to the hallway. As he pulls the door closed, he says, "I'll be right here, Annie. I'm not going anywhere."

For now, I think. Too bad that doesn't feel like nearly long enough.

CHAPTER 6
ARROW

IT'S NEARLY five o'clock by the time Annie and I leave campus.

Her studio was untouched, so she grabbed her laptop while I looked around. I inspected the doors and couldn't see anything unusual. The airflow gap between the floor and the door was more than wide enough for someone to shove a letter underneath without much effort at all. At most, someone would have to slow down and slouch and bam…slide the note and disappear.

We're both quiet as she drives back toward the strip mall, but I'm sure it's for very different reasons. She's got a small suitcase in the back seat containing maybe a week's worth of clothes and toiletries.

"Are there any friends you can stay with?" When I finally break the silence, my question seems to startle her. She jumps a bit but then eases back in the driver's seat.

"Yes, but no," she says. She peeks up in the rearview

again. I notice it because I've been doing the same ever since we left campus.

"No one's following us. I've been watching," I tell her.

"You're probably right," she sighs and shakes her head. "I can't bring that kind of danger around my friends. It wouldn't be fair."

"Annie…" I rub the slight headache forming behind my eyebrows. "Your father should know what's going on with you. Have you thought about—"

We're approaching a red light, but she jams her foot on the brake a little too hard. We both lurch forward against our seat belts.

"No," she says quietly. "Not yet. Not now. You don't know what he's going through, Josh. I can't…I can't. Not now."

The tension pouring from Annie is something different, new. She's angry, defeated. And I can't say I blame her. But every time I bring up her father, she shuts down hard.

If my years of discovering people's secrets have taught me anything, it's that strong emotions are signals. There is more to the story than what she's telling me, you don't have to be a PI to get that.

But whether her reaction every time I bring up her father has anything to do with the letters she's receiving…I have a lot of digging to do. And I just hope she's ready for whatever I might uncover.

A loud rumble from her stomach lightens the mood a bit.

"Same," I say, chuckling. "You want to grab something on the way back to my office? My treat. You've spent enough of your money for one day."

She doesn't respond but gives me a look that I can't interpret. Her eyes are on the road, but for that split second, she glances over at me with something I swear is playful, which reminds me that we're supposed to be together.

"I don't know how I can fake-date you if I don't even know what you eat," I remind her. I adjust my legs as best I can in the small sedan and start listing off cuisine. "Vegan burritos?" I don't wait for her to comment. I just keep talking. "No, you're more of a pizza girl."

My stomach grumbles at the thought of gooey cheese, and I point to my stomach. "That's one vote for pizza, but I'm not picky."

She's grinning now, her cheeks flushed and her shoulders relaxed. "There is a place," she says. "It's my happy place. My favorite restaurant. If you really want to treat me, though, I feel like you should pick the food."

"Hell no," I say, leaning my head back against the seat. "Take me to your happy place."

She laughs then, an almost nervous burst of laughter, and I realize how that might have sounded. Truth is, I don't give a fuck. Annie is sweet, hot, and we have this physical connection that's already something. We've only known each other for a few hours, and while I'm working for her, I won't do anything that we both might regret. But that doesn't mean I'm above teasing her. And touching her—within reason. My mind goes back to holding her in my arms back in her dorm room. She's so goddamn soft, and up close, I could smell the hint of coconut and berry in her hair.

It's been too long since I got laid and even longer since I dated anybody, so I'm going to chalk up my body's reaction to pure need. But there's something about Annie that I like. And I don't like many people.

"So, where you taking me?" I ask, expecting anything from her—a seafood buffet, hole-in-the-wall taco joint. Hell, I'd eat a salad if that's what she wants.

But when we pull into the parking lot of a nearly empty restaurant a few minutes later, I realize there is nothing predictable about this woman.

"You're kidding me," I say, eyeing the sign. "Pancake Circus?"

She turns off the engine and claps her hands. "Yes," she croons. "This is my happy place." She unbuckles the belt and practically leaps out of the car. "And after the day I've had, I need this. Come on."

Pancake Circus looks more like a carnival nightmare than a comfort eatery. The once bright and colorful sign has faded, thanks to God knows how many years baking in the Florida sun. The garish smiles of the circus clowns have mostly melted off, oddly leaving just the dark eyes to stare down at customers as they walk across the pitted asphalt of a parking lot large enough to host a three-ring circus. With real estate as expensive as it is, this place must do good business. I can't imagine how many pancakes they have to sell just to cover the taxes.

But what I can't look away from as we approach the

restaurant is Annie. She's bouncing on her flip-flops, her dark-blond braid over one shoulder, her long legs flexing with every step. She's so excited, it's hard not to crack a grin. I almost break into a jog just to keep up.

"Come on," she calls again, yanking open the glass door.

I shake my head as a blast of ice-cold air conditioning hits me, followed by an assault of smells so good, I have to rethink my previous opinion of the place.

It smells nothing like stale peanuts and carnie sweat in here like I'd envisioned.

Fruit sauces, vanilla, and sizzling bacon hit my nose, and my mouth starts to water before we even hit the hostess stand.

"Mmm, I love it," Annie moans and fans the air in front of her face to take in more of the food smells. She closes her eyes for just a second, and a dreamy look comes over her face until a waitress in exactly the type of kitschy uniform I'd expect from a place like this comes back around from seating another couple.

"Annie." The woman shoves a pair of red plastic glasses up on her nose and grabs two menus so big, the Bible could be printed inside. "Table or booth, my sweet gal?"

"Booth, please," Annie says, a huge grin on her face. "Thank you, Carlene."

Carlene? Clearly, Annie wasn't lying when she said it's her favorite place. She's on a first-name basis with the server, which is more than I can say for myself at any restaurant in the country.

The woman checks a table map of the restaurant, marks off a space with a dry erase marker, and then looks up at me. "Well, holy hell, kid," she barks, lifting perfectly painted-on black brows at me. "Where you been hiding him?"

Annie flushes and steps a little closer to me. She lightly rests her hand in the crook of my arm. "Carlene, this is Josh."

Carlene turns to me, all five-feet-nothing of her, and looks me up and down. "Oh honey, he's tastier than the Big Top Special…"

I can't help but grin at that and casually lace my fingers through Annie's as we follow Carlene to a booth. Can't hurt to keep the lie going, even here, right? At least that's what I tell myself as Carlene looks back at us, shaking her head and grinning from ear to ear.

She drops the menus on the table and watches as I wait for Annie to sit, then slide into the red leather seat across from her.

"You sure you want to do that?" Carlene asks me.

"I'm sorry?" I say, not sure what she means.

Carlene leans down, and I get a whiff of perfume and hair spray. "Annie's a catch," she tells me. "And if she's with you, you are too. I wouldn't sit across from her when you can get right up close there, Josh."

She gives me a friendly squeeze on the shoulder, and I laugh.

"Be back with waters for the table, kids," she calls, then heads out across brightly patterned carpet.

Once we're alone, Annie pushes a menu at me across the table. "Now," she says, her voice light and excited, "I'm not going to tell you what to get, but I will make very strongly worded suggestions based on what you like."

She cracks open the menu—literally cracks because the thing is huge, and the brittle plastic that holds the paper inserts in place is so old and faded, it is breaking in parts. "Okay," she says, not looking at me but skimming the menu. "Are you a breakfast for dinner guy? Or should I look at the entrees?"

As I watch Annie get this enthusiastic about ordering a meal, I can feel a stupid smile crawl across my face. I can't help it. She's fucking gorgeous, and when she's not in fear for her life, she's as light as the Florida sun.

"What are you having?" I ask. To be perfectly honest, I don't care whether I eat a burger or a breakfast burrito. I just want to go along with whatever Annie's doing.

"Okay, okay," she says, pursing her lips into a little bow. "I am normally a breakfast girl, but tonight, I'm… No, no, who am I kidding? We're doing breakfast." She holds up a finger. "First question. Bacon or sausage?"

"Love 'em both," I tell her. "But if I had to pick, bacon."

"Okay, okay," she says again. "Now this is a tough one…fried chicken or bacon?"

"Fuck," I say. "That's a tough one. Both?"

She claps her hands and laughs. "Yes. I knew I liked you. Okay, so let me do the ordering. Do you have any allergies? Any absolute yucks?"

"Absolute yucks…" I echo her words because I can't

believe anyone actually talks like that. But coming from her, it's fucking adorable. "No," I tell her. "Maybe shrimp."

"Oh my God, me too. Crab—yum. Lobster, to die for. But anything that might make it to my plate with its poop still in it…" She shudders. "No thank you." She grabs my menu and pulls it toward her just as Carlene returns with two red plastic glasses filled to the brim with ice water.

"All right, you sexy beasts, whatcha having?" Carlene holds an old-fashioned pad of paper in her hand and a pen that she uses to scrawl our orders.

"Drink?" Annie asks me. "The cotton candy lemonade is actually really good. It's pink but not sweet at all."

"How about just an iced tea?" I say, a tiny bit worried about trusting my stomach to a woman who praises cotton candy lemonade.

Carlene nods. "We've got passion fruit punch, raspberry, and the old-fashioned type." She pokes me in the shoulder with her pen. "Get the raspberry. Trust me. It's absolutely delicious and not sweet at all, or at least not too much."

If I don't have a medical condition by the time I leave this place, I'll be shocked. But I take Carlene's advice and go with the raspberry.

"Elephant Shake for you tonight, babe?" Carlene asks.

Wait. Did I hear that right?

"An elephant shake?" I echo.

"Peanut butter with a tiny peanut butter cookie on

top," Annie explains, looking skyward as if it's the most heavenly thing in the entire universe. "No, you know what? I'm actually feeling like coffee, Carlene. I think I could use the caffeine."

"You got it, gorgeous." Carlene grabs the menus and tucks them under her writing pad, then takes our food order.

I try not to roll my eyes when Annie orders our food, but it's pretty tough when she asks for Corn Dog Chicken and Waffle Pancakes and a Lion Tamer Number Three.

"Annie," I say once Carlene walks off. "If you want to fire me, you can just say it. No need to kill me with circus food."

She shakes her head, a sweet smile on her lips. "If this isn't the best meal you've eaten all month, I'll pay for dinner," she vows. But then she grows serious. "Don't even talk about me firing you. I don't know what I would have done without you today."

She looks down at the table where her fingers are laced together tightly.

"Can we talk?" I ask. "Real talk?"

Those sea-blue eyes meet mine and she nods. "Yeah, of course. What happens now?"

"We find you someplace safe to stay for at least tonight. Tomorrow, I start digging."

She shakes her head. "But where? How? Don't I have to go back to school? I mean, if whoever broke in to my room is the same person who is sending...you know... Then...shouldn't I be at school to get the next letter?"

I lean forward on my elbows and lower my voice. "Annie, we have to assume whoever is leaving the notes is the person who broke in to your room. And I don't think there's any question that whoever is behind all this is intimately familiar with your schedule. I don't think you lost your keys, Annie. I think someone took them."

She leans back against the booth as her eyes widen.

I reach across the table for her hands. "Uh, babe…" I remind her of our cover story. "Try not to look so freaked out, okay? You're safe with me."

She squeezes my hand, and I meet her eyes until her breathing slows. She pulls her hands from mine and clenches her fists in her lap. Just because I can't see them under the booth doesn't mean I don't know she's panicking.

"Listen," I tell her. "Let's play out the scenarios. Best case, it's one person with an ax to grind against you. Maybe it has to do with you getting into the school, maybe not. The fact is, the situation is escalating. The letters started out accusing. Then they made a demand. You got the last letter this morning? Before or after the keys went missing?"

She swallows hard and schools her face into a happy grin as Carlene brings us back our drinks. She sets a large mug of steaming coffee in front of Annie and an enormous glass of raspberry tea in front of me. Then she puts her hands on her hips. "Go on," she says, nodding at me. "Tell me that ain't the best damn tea you've had."

I drag my gaze away from Annie and take a sip of

the tea, praying it doesn't taste like puddle water. The reaction I have when I swallow that first taste is sincere.

"Carlene, if everything in this place is that good, I'm going to ask you to marry me." I take another long sip while Carlene cackles and sets a bowl full of flavored creamers and a sugar dispenser in front of Annie.

"This one's a keeper," she says, cocking her head toward me.

"I think so too," Annie says softly, her face warming.

When Carlene leaves us again, I pick up where we left off. "Annie," I start, "I think there's no other way to look at this. You're in danger. There is someone who knows your routine at school, has access to you. The guy or woman, because it could be a woman, blends in. Looks like he or she belongs there. You can't trust anyone on that campus or anyone affiliated with it."

She looks down, and a single tear drips from her cheek onto the table. It crushes my heart into a million fucking pieces.

"Hey," I say, tapping a finger on the table.

I want to reach out. I want to take her hands again and hold them. Reassure her. But that's a dangerous impulse. I've already let things get too real between us.

Us dating is a lie, a game we're playing. A way for me to explain my presence in her life so I can keep her safe.

What I feel when I touch Annie is the opposite of safe. That's how I know I have to dial things back.

I swipe at the beads of water on the outside of my glass so the urge to touch her doesn't take over. "It's all right. We're going to figure this out, Annie. We're going to go to the police and make a report. About both the break-in in your room and the letters."

"And then what?" she asks miserably. "I had the money to pay you for ten hours, Josh. And that's only because you are practically giving away your time. Now that I have to find another place to stay..." She trails off, shaking her head. "Maybe I should just give them what they want. Maybe...I should drop out of school."

I'd be lying if I said the thought hadn't crossed my mind. But first, I need to know how important this program really is to her. Maybe if I understand why it matters so much, I'll be able to understand why it means so much to whoever is harassing her. And that's if we're even on the right track with that.

For all I know, the letters have nothing to do with the program she's in. The lack of campus security means literally anyone with a grudge against Annie could be tormenting her.

"Annie," I say, "why is this program so important? Let's start there. I don't know a damn thing about art, so school me."

My pun brings a half smile to her face. She sips her coffee and lets out a pleasurable sigh. "It's the weirdest thing, grad school," she says. "I feel like the biggest hurdle is feeling like you're good enough to get in. My family wasn't super educated. Dad went to community college and then got an undergrad degree while he worked in manufacturing. He had management aspirations and they paid for college, but I'm sure he wouldn't have gone, otherwise. My mom..."

A shadow crosses her face as she talks about her mom.

"Mom started working as a legal secretary right out of high school. She was an actual secretary, though, you know? She answered calls and greeted guests. I think the law office environment is what made my dad think of being a lawyer after she passed. Mom loved her job. The firm she worked at handled only immigration cases, and Mom was just so good with people. She loved that what they did there really helped people solve problems and change their lives. At least, that's what my dad has always told me."

As she talks, she sorts the creamers into piles on the table, stacking them by flavor. It's a nervous habit, I think, but it's cute. I can see her adjusting and twisting the plastic cups so the labels all face different directions. It's like she's making art with the most colorful thing at hand.

The urge to touch her, to hold her hand, comes over me, but I grab my iced tea and take a long drink. I need to cool off.

"So anyway," she continues, "I fell in love with art while Dad was in law school. But to be the kind of artist that sells work or has gallery shows… It's not easy. You need to network and know all sorts of people. And you know, it takes time to produce the art itself. I thought grad school would give me the space and time to invest fully in everything I need to do to make this a career, but maybe this isn't what I was meant to do after all."

"Can I see it?" I ask. "Your art?"

Annie's face lights up like I've shined a spotlight on

her. "Seriously? Heck yeah." She sets her cell phone on the table and swipes to open an album of photos. "This is just stuff I've made since school started," she says. "If you keep scrolling, you can tell by the background what's older. That's the kitchen table in my old apartment, which I never actually ate on." She laughs and hands me her phone.

I pick it up and swipe through the images, stunned at what I'm seeing. "What is this?" I ask her. "You made these?"

I can't tell the difference between textile art and a kitchen towel, but what I'm seeing is blowing my mind. Photo after photo captures lifelike images of things painted but not with paint. Sewn with thread or scraps of fabric.

"This shit looks real," I tell her, unable to hold back the awe in my voice. "How do you do it?"

She looks pleased with my compliments. Her smile is almost as big as when she announced we were going to her happy place. She shrugs as if it's no big deal, but I can't stop staring.

"I can hardly sign my own name legibly, but this… Fuck, Annie. I can't believe there's a damn thing they could teach you in that program that you're not already doing. You're goddamn talented."

She's still preening under my praise when she slides out of her side of the booth and comes around to sit beside me. "Look," she says. "This is my problem."

I'm still holding the phone, but she reaches over my hand and swipes through the images with a finger.

"This," she says, "embroidered still life. Fruit in a bowl. Nothing fancy."

"But it's fucking cool." I can't see how anyone could look at apples, bananas, and a pineapple that look textural and real, made out of fucking threads, and not be impressed.

"But then this." She swipes to a face, a portrait in black, white, and grays. The picture looks dated, like it could have been taken in the seventies. But again, it's not a picture. It's a woman in a convertible car with a pair of sunglasses made from scraps of leather and fabric. I think when I use my fingers to zoom into the detail, there are buttons and other small metal pieces in the piece as well. "And then this one."

The next thing she shows me, I don't know what to think. It's a three-dimensional rose that looks like it's growing from a cracked mirror. It gives off a darker vibe. The edges of the bright red rose are wine-colored and curled like the rose is dying.

"This is my problem." She takes the phone back, but she doesn't return to her side of the booth. Her arm lightly brushes mine, and a wave of heat travels through my body. "I don't have a message. A brand. Any collection I make would be a mishmash of things that are meaningful to me. But that's the difference between craft-fair artists and fine artists. Consumers might buy my stuff, but not galleries. Not collectors. I'm not trying to shit on anyone's art. It's a miracle when someone is willing to pay their hard-earned money for art in any form and at any price." She sighs, and unless I'm imagining it, I feel the heat of her thigh close to mine. "I was hoping to discover myself in school. Find my voice, so to speak."

Just then, Carlene bustles over carrying a huge tray weighed down with plates. "Oh, I like the looks of this," she says, waggling dark brows at us. "You two are some kind of cute together." She sets down a platter-sized plate in front of me and a second in front of Annie. "Enjoy, kids," she says. She tucks the tray under an arm and points at me. "You need anything, you holler." She sets a stack of paper napkins on the table and leaves us.

Annie claps her hands and rubs them together. "Now, the real fun begins." She looks at me shyly and then slips back around to her side of the booth.

I shove her plate toward her side of the table and then unwrap my fork and knife. "Holy shit," I say, breathing deep. "This is the Corn Dog Chicken and Waffle Pancakes?"

She nods, her expression gleeful. Like a kid at the circus. "That coating on the chicken," she says, pointing to the four fried chicken drumsticks on my plate, "is just like the batter on a corn dog. And the waffle pancake is really a thick, cornmeal pancake lightly pressed in a waffle maker to give it those little nooks for texture. This…"

She reaches across the table and lifts up a tiny stainless-steel pitcher that sits between the most gorgeous golden-brown waffle-looking thing and the chicken.

"This is hot honey. The waffle is sprinkled with powdered sugar, but I slather this stuff on the waffle and then dip the chicken into it. It's so good."

She pushes her plate toward me. "And you've got to try this. Lion Tamer Number Three is the bacon option, but you can get Lion Tamer with steak or ham steak or even deep-fried catfish."

The Lion Tamer is basically a giant scramble with an obscene amount of meat in it. Over my protests, Annie scoops up a forkful of her food that looks like it contains about a pound of bacon and drops it on my plate.

The conversation lulls as we eat, and I shock myself by polishing off my entire meal. I'm going to need to double my time at the gym after this.

Carlene brings Annie a to-go box and hands me the check, and I pay for dinner like the good boyfriend she believes I am. And then, far too soon, it's time to get Annie settled in someplace for the night.

CHAPTER 7
ANNIE

I PULL into the parking lot of the Palm Dream hotel. It's definitely not looking like a dream stay is ahead of me, but the place is cheap and met all of Josh's requirements—lobby staffed overnight, no external access to the rooms. He wanted a hotel that limited parking to registered guests only, but that would have taken such a huge chunk out of my budget that we agreed this nondescript hotel would do for one night.

He pulls into a spot at the opposite end of the lot and turns off his engine. As we agreed, I take my time gathering my things from my trunk and back seat, and when he texts me that it's all clear, I head into the lobby. He follows just a few seconds behind.

"Hey," he says, putting an arm over my shoulder. "Babe, you shouldn't have brought in all the bags."

He takes my suitcase from me, and for a second, it's like he's actually mine and we are checking in to a hotel for a sweet little getaway. But the reality of why I'm here is too scary. I can't indulge even the most escapist fantasy for long.

"Thanks...uh, babe," I tell him, liking way too much how the endearment feels on my lips.

"Parking was good," he tells me. "All ready to check in?"

Josh and I made a plan when I brought him back to his office. He would follow me in his truck and let me unload the bags and head into the hotel while he stayed back to watch for any signs that I'd been followed. It was probably overkill. We both knew that. There was no one in the parking lot of his office, so I wasn't really worried I was being followed until Josh mentioned how easy it would be for someone to put a tracking device on my car.

Ever since he mentioned the tracker, I haven't been able to relax. My Lion Tamer dinner feels like a lead brick in my stomach, and all I want to do is go home.

The problem is, I don't know where home is now.

My dorm room was too new to really feel like my own place. I haven't lived with my dad for a couple of years, and I gave up my apartment.

I don't think I have felt quite so alone in a long time.

And when the desk clerk hands Josh and me electronic keycards, the Palm Dream becomes my temporary home.

Josh takes his credit card back from the hotel manager and loops an arm around my waist. They did not ask for my name or ID, so that's just one more layer of anonymity that should help me sleep better tonight.

Should, but I doubt it.

I'm already realizing that if someone has a tracker on my car—because despite Josh's thorough search before we left his office, I'm still not completely sure there isn't—if I walk out of my room for ice or when I go to leave in the morning, I'm as good as exposed.

Funny how hours ago, when I met Josh, I was curious about whether a PI could help me. Now I'm afraid of what I'll do without him.

We walk to the elevator, and he presses the button. Once we're alone inside, he releases me and gets down to business.

"The reservation is under my name and credit card, so even if someone tracks you here, connecting you to my name will be tough."

I nod, but his body is tense, and his voice sounds strained. He's taking the threat to my safety as seriously as I am, and while that should make me feel better, it only makes me more aware that I've been so clueless.

I thought those letters were a prank. A joke. Maybe even intended for someone else entirely and not me. But now? I feel like I have a giant bull's-eye on my back.

When the door opens on the third floor, Josh looks into the hallway, then grabs my suitcase, and leads the way out. We don't say the room number aloud but follow the signs to Room 312. He waits while I swipe my keycard and watches the little green light go on to show that I can enter.

I walk in, and Josh lets the door close behind me, then he swipes his key to test that it works.

"Always check every key," he says as he comes

inside. "They're coded for each guest, but things go wrong. Better safe than…" He trails off.

"I know," I say quietly.

He walks through the room, past the king-sized bed, and looks out the windows. The room overlooks the parking lot, which he doesn't love, but the windows are locked and there doesn't seem to be any way someone could easily access the room from the outside. No balcony. No visible fire escape. There's no adjoining room connected by a pass-through door, so really, I couldn't ask for much more in a hotel room.

Except to not have to stay here alone.

Josh sets my suitcase up on the luggage rack and then shoves his hands into his pockets. He rocks back on his feet like he realizes it's time to go but he wants to stay. Or maybe that's just how I feel. I don't know anymore. We've known each other one day, and yet I trust myself with him completely. I feel all the more attached to him because I know that, right now, I have no one else I can go to.

"Annie," he says quietly. "I want you to lock the door—the dead bolt and the safety latch—when I go, okay? And put a chair in front of the door if it makes you feel safer. You should be okay here overnight."

"I will," I assure him, trying to rally all my confidence and courage. "Yeah. I…I'll be okay. You've done so much for me. Thank you. I'll pay you back for the hotel."

He gives me a smile that's part sexy, part teasing, and it melts all my anxiety away. "Just don't go bananas on the minibar, or at least warn me if you plan to max out my credit card."

I lean forward and give him a playful swat on the chest, but he catches my hand with his.

He squeezes my hand firmly. "You're going to be okay, babe." He grins again and then releases my hand far too soon. I could have used at least another few minutes of his reassuring touch.

"I will," I say.

He checks his phone and rubs his eyes. "I'm going home to get some sleep," he says. "Nobody knows you're here, Annie. But if anything weird happens, don't answer the door. Call the front desk. Call me. Call the police. Maybe call the cops first, but definitely call me. Okay?"

I nod. "I will. Thank you."

"Check in with me first thing in the morning," he says, covering his mouth as he yawns. "I'll come by and follow you to school, and we can make a plan for what comes next. Deal?"

"Deal."

He looks at me with an expression I can't really interpret, but I feel some kind of way I can't really understand. So we're quite the fake couple, I guess. I mean, I know I'm stressed that he's leaving. But I feel a closeness with him that, well, doesn't make any sense.

Maybe it's because he's the only one I have to lean on right now, but that's literally what I want more than anything. To lean against his chest and fall asleep feeling safe. Not alone.

Even weirder, I want to know more about him. He's

asked about my art, my family, and my life. But I don't know anything about him, and now most definitely does not feel like the time.

"When this is all over," he says, raking a hand through his hair, "I'm definitely going back to Pancake Circus."

I blurt out a really awkward laugh because that surprises me. "You liked it?" I ask.

"It might just become my new happy place," he says, the corners of his lips curling. "Carlene's not going to like me very much if I go without you," he adds.

"I'm in," I say, maybe a little too quickly. "Next time, Lion Tamer Number Two. I hope you're ready for all that sausage."

As it hits me how suggestive and awkward what I said is, I shake my head and almost cry tears, I'm laughing so hard. "I better get to sleep," I say. "Before I say something that makes you want to fire me as a client."

"Not going to happen," he says quietly, but then he turns and unlocks the door. "Annie," he says, holding up his phone. "Lock the door behind me. And you call if anything happens, okay?"

I nod. "I think you've already burned through the ten hours of time I hired you for," I say quietly.

"You let me keep track of my time." He's standing in the hall. My hand is on the doorknob. "Good night, Annie," he says. "I'm going to wait until I hear you lock the door. Knock once when you're all secure."

"Good night, Josh." I close the door, fasten both locks, and knock once against the door.

And then, he's gone.

I walk over to the window and peek through the curtains. No one's out there at this time of night. Crap, it's almost nine. Josh and I really have spent like ten hours together. It seems like so much more and so much less all at the same time.

It's hitting me how exhausted I am when I see Josh walk past my car and look up at my window. He doesn't wave, but I'm sure he sees me because when he gets into his truck, he flashes the lights once and then drives away.

Now, he's really gone.

Out of sight. Out of reach.

I'm totally alone.

I rub the back of my neck and realize I am wrecked. I need a bath and to crash in this ultra-big bed that makes the barely more than a twin mattress that lost its life in my dorm room today look like a joke.

What am I really hoping to accomplish in art school anyway? Finding myself as an artist? If that's something I haven't done by the age of twenty-five, how much longer will that take? I don't have a major social message to share. I just want to create beautiful things that move and inspire people.

As I dig through my luggage for my water bottle and pajamas, I realize that maybe I'm not that different from my father. He never wanted to be a high-powered lawyer, driving fancy cars and dazzling opponents in the courtroom. He wanted to make a stable living doing real, consistent, valuable work.

That's why this opportunity means so much to me. As much as I love my dad, I don't think he's really happy. The last year, especially, he's been off.

I've been worried he's hiding some kind of problem from me. Maybe that's why he sent me off to school to pursue my dreams. I thought maybe he, too, was feeling his mortality. How short and fragile life could be.

Working in his real estate firm would have been a stable income, but was it the life I was meant to live? Nope.

I figured if Dad is sick or in some kind of trouble, sending me off to school was his way of giving me the chance to have more.

I brush my teeth and shake out my hair, then run the water for a bath. I climb in and let myself soak, draining the entire hotel-issued plastic container of shower gel into the running water. The gel bubbles up nicely, and I lie back in the tub until my hair mermaids around me.

I close my eyes and think of my mother. My father. School. I can't figure any of it out. Not tonight.

I turn on the water and scrub my hair with the hotel shampoo and wish I'd thought to unpack my own conditioner to work through my long strands, but that's fine. This isn't about anything more than washing the grime and sweat and fear of the day away.

I climb out of the bathtub when I hear the text alert on my phone chime. I wrap myself in a fluffy towel and pad barefoot to the bed where I left my phone.

I grin when I see the message.

Neveah: Hey, girl. Checking in on you.

I'll text her back once I'm settled in bed, and we'll have a good chat. I head back to the bathroom and massage lotion into my legs and arms, then slip into my shorts and the button-down cotton top covered with cupcakes that I brought to sleep in.

I brush out my wet hair and put a towel over my shoulders to catch the spare drips because there is no way I'm blow-drying this mess right now. I want to stretch out on the fluffy bed and text the one friend who already knows I've had a shit day. I won't have to relive it and can just shoot the shit with her.

Before I even make it back to my bed, my phone's pinging again. I crawl across the smooth white duvet and lean back against a mountain of pillows. I'm feeling more relaxed, and I'm hopeful that I can actually get some good sleep tonight.

I swipe the touchscreen and see I have another message from Neveah.

Annie Hannie, where you at? I just came down to your room to check on you, but you didn't answer. You home with your dad?

I type a yawn face emoji and then a message.

So wiped, but I'm hoping to get some good sleep tonight. I'll be back tomorrow to start cleaning up. How's your commission coming?

We text a little about the project she's been working

on for the commission June referred her for, when Neveah asks again.

Girl, where you spending the night? With that Josh guy? Who is he? Why didn't you tell me you had somebody so hot?

I grin and send back a flame emoji.

He is hot, isn't he? I reply.

Smokin', she says.

That's all that comes through for a minute, and I'm about to text her another question about her commission. And really, I want to pick her brain about how she figured out what her message was going to be, what kind of statement her art was going to make, but another text comes through before I finish typing.

Annie, I think you should come back to campus. If you're worried, you can crash for the night in my room. I'd feel better knowing where you are. That you're safe.

I'm safe, I text back. *Pinkie promise. I'll be back tomorrow. Needed a break from the mess and all the weirdness.*

I'm starting to get a strange vibe, but I can't exactly explain why. She's asked a bunch of times where I am, and while I would expect a friend to be worried, it's also pretty clear that I'm not going to say where I'm staying tonight.

I'm not sure why Neveah keeps asking. She's my RA, so when I'm on campus, I'm technically her responsibility, but not really. She's more like a floor counselor or guide than anything. And I'm an adult student. It's not like I can't spend every night off campus with my boyfriend if I choose. Even if that's not where I am, that's where I hope Neveah thinks I am.

Will you at least tell me this Josh guy's last name? And

let me know for sure you're with him? I'm worried, girl. The mess in your room isn't cool. Even if it was just a shitty prank, I want to know my girl's safe.

Something about her asking for Josh's last name sets my teeth on edge. I get up from the bed and peek out into the parking lot. Nothing seems any different. Everything is dark.

I'm safe, I text back. *Going to crash. Catch up on campus tomorrow.*

I'm still holding the phone when it rings. The caller ID says it's Neveah.

All I can think about is what Josh said today. Whoever is sending these letters has access to me. Close access. They would blend in, and I'd never even suspect they'd stolen my keys.

It can't be her, I think. She can't have anything to do with what's going on. She's my friend. Isn't she?

I'm getting paranoid, but who the hell could blame me?

My heart starts banging in my chest, and I realize that if someone has a tracker on my car, maybe there could be some way to track me using my phone too. I don't know. I'm a freaking artist not a PI. I wonder for a minute if I should text Josh and ask him. Is it safe to answer the phone?

I don't really know Neveah. Not any better than I know anyone else at school. But why would she call me when I said I was wiped and going to bed?

Maybe she was trying to be a good friend. Maybe she was trying to be a supportive RA.

All I know is that right now, the only person I trust in the world is Josh.

My hand starts to shake so hard I drop the phone, and it hits the hotel carpet.

"Shit." I pick it up and flip the ringer to silent.

I plug my phone into the charger, and once the call goes to voice mail, I turn the ringer back on. Neveah doesn't leave a message, but she doesn't call back or text again. I sit awake on the bed, worrying myself into a throbbing headache until my hair is dry.

By the time midnight rolls around, my eyes are burning, my hair is a rumpled mess, and I have made a nest of pillows around me in the king-sized bed.

I close my eyes and imagine Josh's arms around me. That brings me some comfort and a little more than some throbbing between my legs, but I leave the lights on.

There's no chance I'm getting much sleep tonight.

CHAPTER 8
ARROW

BY EIGHT, I'm at my desk and wondering if I should check on Annie. I know I should let her sleep. She's a full-time student, something I've never been, so for all I know, she sleeps until noon and works through the night. I walk over to the coffeemaker I keep in my office and brew up a full pot.

I feel like I hardly slept a wink last night. When I wasn't checking my phone for texts, my dreams were more than stimulating. It's unnerving, the effect Annie has had on me. I have other clients and other work to do, so I put the golden-legged artist out of my mind and log in to my email.

Yeah, scratch that. I have no other clients. No other work. More of the same. Empty inbox. I do have a message from one of the guys I work with at an insurance company, but the news is worse than just the usual —no, we don't have any new cases right now.

Mike tells me the insurance company he works for is going to start using more in-house investigators for their suspected workers' comp fraud cases. Something about standardizing training and procedures to ensure more consistent investigation methods across the open cases.

Great.

That's corporate speak that means they want to roll what I do into the jobs of overworked guys who are already on the payroll. It's a cost-cutting measure. That's all that is.

I do good work. Honest work. Some of the cases I've handled have saved the company hundreds of thousands of dollars. Claim payments weren't made—didn't go out the door to people milking their injuries or trying to extend benefits longer than they were entitled to. Those are big wins for the company, considering they don't pay me a percentage of what I save them. They pay me my flat hourly rate plus expenses, which still nets them big gains.

But they don't see it like that.

I storm over to the coffeepot and fill the biggest mug I've got. Looks like there's no reason not to put all my time and energy into Annie.

She's literally all I've got now.

I decide to start my day with research. While I down my coffee, I look up everything I can find, starting with Annie herself. But after an hour, I find very little that I didn't already know. All of her social media profiles are discreet and art-related. She doesn't have any weird engagements on her posts, and even a search of her followers and people who have communicated with her publicly online reveals most are female artists. Which brings me back to my original line of thinking.

The school is the logical tie to what's happening.

I spend another hour researching the school, complaints about the school, crime stats, but nothing. The school is small and doesn't have much of an online footprint. June, her thesis adviser, has a website, so I learn what I can about her. She definitely has had an interesting career. She started out as a sculptor but has been teaching in some capacity for more than twenty years. She has sold work to a number of businesses and hotels but, otherwise, nothing remarkable or revealing.

That brings me to Annie's resident adviser, Neveah. I don't know her last name so I can't do much more than search for information about her on the school site. I don't find anything.

My phone rings, and my heart practically leaps out of my chest. I expect to see Annie's name on the caller ID, but it's just Alice, one of the owners of the building.

"Alice," I say, picking up after the first ring.

"Josh, hon, are you busy this morning? I wanted to drop by with a copy of the new lease. Go over a couple of the terms with you." She sounds like she's got me on speaker.

I imagine her husband Morris is with her. I'm due to renew my lease, and I'm sure the rate's going up. When Morris and Alice bought this strip mall, they needed to fill it, so they put a lot of tenant-friendly terms in the initial lease. But they warned me that could change. And like anything that's going to cost me money, these changes are not ones I'm ready for.

My lease renews in ninety days, and if I can't turn things around, I'm not sure I can re-sign. I don't have to provide any notice if I decide not to renew, but Alice and Morris have to give me notice of the changes coming.

I guess right now is my notice.

"Come on by," I tell Alice, feeling the coffee slosh around in my gut. "I'll be here."

I hang up the phone and walk into the tiny office bathroom to dump the last of my now-cold coffee down the sink. I splash water on my face, wash my hands, and smooth back my hair. The guy looking back at me has one thing going for him—he works.

I'm tenacious and smart, but that means fuck all if I don't have any clients. Well, more than just Annie.

Morris and Alice arrive a few minutes later. I clap Morris on the back and shake his hand while I give Alice a smile.

She's a sweet lady. I'm the only tenant they have who isn't somehow in the MC that her husband runs with Tiny. Alice never makes me feel like an outsider. I'm friends with Leo, who's not fully patched in, as well as Lia, Tiny's daughter. But being friends doesn't bring me close enough to feel like they ever fully trust me.

"How's business, man?" Morris looks comically suburban in his tight black golf shirt. He's got kids now —Zoey, Alice's daughter from a previous relationship— and they recently added another little one to the family, another girl just a few months younger than Leo and Lia's son, Rider.

Morris stretches his thick legs out in front of him and pushes the chair back a few feet from the desk.

"Business as usual," I tell him, not willing to reveal anything that will make my landlords worry about my ability to renew. We'll all cross that bridge when and if we have to.

"Glad to hear it." Morris has a file folder in his heavily tattooed hands. He sets it on the desk, but I'm not quite ready to get the bad news yet.

"How're the kids?" I ask, not really directing the question to him or Alice, but both. "I saw Rider yesterday." I shake my head. "They grow up fast."

I don't know what the hell to say to parents. They grow up fast. The kids are cute. I don't have much in the way of family anymore, and none of my buddies have kids.

To me, Rider's a cute, screaming mess of juice and snot. Half the time when I see the kid, he's waddling like he's got a diaper full of shit. The rest of the time, he's moving so fast, I don't get how legs that tiny can propel a body that quickly.

It's not that I don't like kids. There's nothing wrong with them—they're just not my people.

Morris's grizzled beard softens as he grins. He laces his fingers together behind his head and smiles. "Girl dad, best job on earth," he says.

"And you're the best at what you do." Alice leans down and kisses Morris's cheek.

I lean forward and reach for the file folder. "So, what's the damage?" I ask, moving on to the business at hand.

Before any of us can start talking, the front door to my office flies open.

"Josh! Josh!"

I recognize the voice and leap from my chair. "Excuse me one sec."

I hurry into the lobby where Annie is clutching a piece of paper in her hands. She's pale, and soft smudges under her eyes make her look like she's slept about as much as I did.

"Annie." I rush up to her and instinctively take hold of her arms. "What happened? Are you okay?"

She's trembling so hard, I can't imagine what the fuck has got her so worked up. And worse, why she didn't fucking call.

"Talk to me," I say, peering down into her face. "Whatever it is, I'll take care of you. Just tell me what happened."

"They found me," she squeaks out, the hand that's gripping the letter trembling. "But it's so much worse. Josh, they found you."

I release her arms and take the letter from her hand. In the same printing I remember from the other letters is a simple message.

Annie, you're pathetic. Josh can't stop what's coming for you.

I start to see red as rage erupts from my gut. "Where was this? Where did you find this?"

"Tucked under my wipers," she says. "That's why I didn't call. I went out to my car after I checked out. I was planning on texting you and heading into school, but I saw this under my wipers and freaked the fuck out."

"Fuck," I curse and press at the splitting pain behind my brows with two fingers. "Tell me everything. What happened last night. Who you've talked to, where you've been."

She tells me in a shaky voice about Neveah, texting and calling at the hotel last night. How she went to sleep but kept dreaming that Neveah would show up at the door looking for her.

"And then this morning, my father called me." She looks so young and so scared, I want to pull her close, protect her from whatever shitstain is tormenting her.

"What'd your dad say?" I demand. "Does he know what happened in the dorm?" I realize Alice and Morris are waiting for me, but this *can't* wait.

"It was so weird, Josh," she tells me, sounding lost. "He asked me if everything was okay at school. I told him, yeah, everything was great. I didn't say anything about the dorm or the letters. Nothing. He said he was between meetings, but before he hung up, he told me he slept better at night knowing I'm safe at school. He sounded weird. Like he wasn't alone. It just left me with the weirdest feeling." She looks up at me, tears in her eyes. "Josh, do you think my dad put a tracker on my car? Why would he do that? But how did the letter get on my car in the hotel lot? How do they know your name?"

She's full-body trembling now, and I have to admit, I have all the same questions.

If they know who I am, that means they know she's

hired me. That means not only the hotel, but my office, my home… Any place that I once considered secure might be compromised.

"Fuck," I say, and when the reality of what I'm feeling crosses my face, Annie bursts into tears.

"I'm so sorry. I don't even know why this is happening."

I do it then. I open my arms, and she crashes against my chest, wrapping her arms tight around my waist.

"I'm so scared," she says, her breath warm against my shirt. "And angry and paranoid. I brought this down on you. I don't understand. I just don't get it."

I hold her tight and press my chin to the top of her head. "It's going to be all right. We're going to work this out, I promise."

A throat clearing behind me has me turning my neck, but I don't release Annie.

"Josh, we can come back another time," Morris says at the same time Alice asks, "Who is this? Is everything okay?"

Annie pulls back a little and then a look of horror comes over her face. "Oh my God, you're busy," she says, looking from Morris to Alice. "I never even thought you'd be with clients, I'm so, so sorry…"

"Annie, these are my landlords. It's okay."

Annie smooths down the front of a purple-patterned flowy dress that hugs her tits and ties around the back of her neck. Her hair is loose and free, and she's wearing flip-flops again. She wipes the tears from her face. "I'm not usually this much of a wreck," she says.

"I'm in a bit of trouble, but I'm sure you're used to that."

"We can come back later, Arrow," Morris says, using the nickname most of my friends and the MC guys call me. "Sorry for your troubles, miss."

Morris looks ready to haul ass out of there, but Annie shakes her head. "No, please. I can…I can wait. I can't go home anyway. I…I can't go anywhere."

I lift her chin so her eyes meet mine. "You'll be safe here. Just sit at my desk and don't talk to anyone or leave this office until I'm done. You got me?"

She nods. "Are you sure?"

I point to the desk where I met with her yesterday. "I'll be quick. Then I'll take you for some coffee and we'll figure this out."

My mind is already spinning with shit we have to do. But first, I need to get Morris and Alice taken care of.

"Come on back," I tell them. "Annie, don't leave my sight, babe."

When I say babe, the light finally comes back into her face. She smiles and nods, then sits in the chair behind the desk facing the door.

Smart girl.

I close my office door, grateful it has a window so I can see Annie, after Alice and Morris come back inside.

"Josh," Alice says, her voice a mixture of teasing and surprise. "I didn't know you were seeing anyone. Is everything okay?"

I sigh, figuring it's a lot easier to keep up the charade that I'm dating Annie than it would be to explain it. "I'm helping her with what I think is an emerging stalking situation," I tell them. "We'd thought whoever it is didn't know about me, but…" I motion toward Annie. "She found out this morning that's not the case. That means she can't go home. And now, well…"

I rake a hand through my hair and curse.

"Looks like my home and office address have been compromised. I don't know if there's a threat to me personally, but you might want to notify the other tenants to be cautious. Until this gets sorted, I don't know what kind of danger she or I might be in."

"Fuck it, Arrow. I don't like that one bit." Morris's expression is dark. "My wife is here alone most days." He scratches his fingers through his gray stubble. "What can we do?"

I look from him to Alice and back. "What do you mean?"

The question takes me by surprise. I'm not friends with Morris and Alice. While I get that they want to secure the property, there have been cameras on the premises since Alice's ex tried to burn the damn place down right after they bought it. And since my office is right next to Alice's, I can confirm I've seen the setup. The cameras work. Anything that happens, there will be a record of it.

But cameras only catch what they can. They don't stop crimes from happening. If I were Morris right now, I'd be worried sick and wanting to help too.

Morris looks at Alice. "We could post a fake eviction

notice on the door. Make this stalker fuck think Josh doesn't work here anymore."

The idea has merit, but I don't like the idea of any potential clients who show up thinking I got evicted. That'll drive the last nail in the coffin of my business for sure.

"I don't know about that, man," I say.

"What if you put a sign on the door that says 'Out of town for family emergency. Accepting phone calls only at this time'?" Alice looks more troubled than I've ever seen her. She is twisting halfway in her chair, one eye trained on Annie.

"I like that," I say. "That could work. That way, if anyone comes here, it might stop them from trying anything."

Morris nods. "I'll get a couple of the brothers down here. Crow's working now, but Eagle and Dog can spare the time. Tiny won't let anything happen with his baby girl and grandson right here."

For the first time since I've known these guys, I see the power of the brotherhood. I don't have anyone to call at a time like this. No one to watch my back. I don't mind being a lone wolf, but I can't deny that I want the kind of help the guys can bring to this situation.

"Seriously appreciate that, man," I tell him.

We spend a few minutes going over the changes in the lease, while Alice continues to look like she wants to go hug Annie. I know that feeling all too well.

When we finish, Morris stands and shakes my hand, leaving a copy of the new lease on my desk. "You know the deal, man. Just get the signed copy back to us by the time the lease turns over. Unless you're not planning to stay, then let us know when you can."

I thank him again and get up from my chair. "Can I ask a favor? You think we could leave Annie's car in the lot here for a while? I suspect she's got a tracker installed on it, and until I have a chance to look it over and find the fucking thing, I'd like to keep the car some-place Annie and I won't be."

"Josh," Alice says quietly. "What happens now? Where will you and Annie go?"

I pinch my nose between my thumb and forefinger. "I haven't gotten that far yet."

And it's true. I know we can't stay here, she can't go back to the dorms, and I'm going to bet my condo won't be any more secure. If this asshole knows my name, a simple Google search will be all it takes to find me. Property tax records, utilities... As much as I maintain as low a profile as possible, I'm findable. And it looks like this stalker is a little too motivated to get under Annie's skin.

Alice looks at her husband, then strokes his massive, tattooed forearm. "Honey," she says quietly. "Can we talk a second?"

Morris cocks his chin at her but nods. I feel like I'm interrupting a private conversation, so I push back from the chair and motion toward Annie. "I'm going to check on her," I say. "I'll give you two some time."

I close my office door behind me and walk over to the desk at the front of the office. I lean against the side of the reception desk and cross my legs.

"What do you need?" I ask. "Caffeine? Pancakes?"

She laughs, the golden bronze of her bare shoulders shaking. "I don't think I could eat. Maybe we can grab coffee and figure out what to do next?"

I'm about to tell her what I learned this morning, when Alice opens the door to my office. "Josh, Annie," she says, smiling sweetly. "I think we can help."

CHAPTER 9
ANNIE

THE LAST PLACE I ever imagined I'd find myself is on the back of a motorcycle. Which makes the idea of moving in to a motorcycle club compound absolutely ridiculous.

"Is it like on TV?" I ask, looking from Josh to Morris.

While Josh has the sexy bad-boy vibe in spades, Morris looks every bit the craggy, crusty biker. He's attractive—don't get me wrong—with a great body, tattoos, and thick, trim hair that puts him in the silver fox category. The sun lines around his eyes and his work-weathered hands were formed through years of riding the open road.

The massive man takes one look at Alice, bends over, and bursts into full-belly laughter. "Oh gosh, I wish. The Disciples compound looks more like a day care than a club hangout these days."

He wipes the corners of his eyes, and I have to laugh with him. His wife Alice is small and sweet, but that doesn't mean I relish the thought of staying in a man cave full of bikers who don't have wives and kids to go home to.

"Honey, Josh can stay with you. That's not a problem. I assume because his place is compromised, too, that's what you both want." Alice points to Morris. "And this one will kick the ass of any of those guys who even looks at you funny."

Josh is oddly silent about the offer they've made to the two of us, moving into a vacant room in the Disciples compound while Josh continues to work on my case. It's generous. It's practical because it's the last damn place that anyone would think to look for me.

Even with the doubts I have, it's clear I have no better options. Unless I want to completely bankrupt myself in a matter of days, moving from one hotel to another.

"And my car?" I ask. "If I bring that along, won't I just reveal my location to whoever has a tracker on it?"

Josh interrupts then. "Your car can stay here. Anyone who's watching will figure out quick you're not living in this strip mall."

Josh explains that since he's not sure whether I'll be safe, for the next few days, he'll take me to school. As much as I appreciate the offer, I can't afford more of Josh's time. But this is serious. Really serious. It's not only my safety that's at stake, but my future well-being. If I throw every penny I have at Josh, then what?

Sigh. I don't like any of it.

But at this point, both my safety and Josh's are on the line. What other choice do I have? Even if I can't afford to pay him for all his time, we both need a safe place to sleep until this gets sorted out. Or it ends. I shiver at the thought of all the ways this might end, and suddenly living with a bunch of wild bikers sounds a lot more appealing.

"Can I ask how much?" I ask.

"How much?" Morris cocks his chin. "I don't follow you, sweetheart."

"She wants to know how much you'll charge her to stay at the compound," Josh supplies.

Alice looks at Morris, who glowers at me with the kind of menacing look I'd hope he'd turn on anyone who threatened my safety.

"We don't profit off helping our own," Morris grits out. He smacks Josh across the chest. "This guy's not one of us, but he's close enough. What we have is ours to share with whomever we choose. And I'm offering a roof over your head and meals for as long as you both need it. Understand? I don't want to hear another word about money." He waves a hand at me and turns to Josh. "You can take Crow's old room. I'll talk to Tiny. When are you planning on rolling in?"

Josh looks at me, then back at Morris. "You think Tiny's going to go for this?"

Morris lifts his brows, and that ends the conversation.

"This afternoon," Josh confirms. "We have some things to take care of, but we'll move in today."

Morris and Josh talk a bit about logistics while Alice comes and loops a hand around my arm. "Annie, I know you don't know me, but the MC is family. And that makes anyone they take under their wing family too." She gives me a warm squeeze and then releases me. "You and Josh should come by our house for dinner sometime, meet my little ones. I have a ten-year-old and a one-year-old. If that doesn't tell you everything you need to know about our life…"

I smile. "I'd love that, thank you." And even though I don't know this woman from Adam, I mean it. The invitation seems sincere, and I could use some genuine friends right now.

"All right, man." Morris claps Josh hard on the shoulder and then walks up to me and offers me his hand. "Great meeting you, darlin'," he says. "I'll see you at the compound."

Alice and Morris head out, leaving Josh and me alone. I don't know what to say, and for a moment, it seems like Josh doesn't either.

Things have changed.

We're not just pretending to be a couple so no one asks questions. We're continuing a lie that is just going to keep growing.

While at the same time, the reality of why we're doing this is taking me to a dark place. I drop into a chair, grip my knees with my hands, and take a long, deep breath.

"Annie, are you okay? We can put the brakes on this plan anytime. You just say the word." His brows are knitted together, and I am overcome with gratitude that he's giving me a choice.

Truth is, I don't know if I'm okay. I don't know what I did to get myself into this situation. I'm a nobody. A basic person who wanted to get a degree, make some art, and figure out who I am.

Now there's a tracker on my car, a stalker on my tail, and I'm about to move in to a compound with biker outlaws.

"Josh, I...I don't even know what to say. I got you into this..." I lace my fingers together and glance down. "I'm grateful there's a place we can both go to be safe. But..." I look up and meet his melted-chocolate eyes, "I can't take their charity. I can cook and clean. I can make myself useful. You didn't sign up for this. You gave me a deal on ten hours of your time, and now look." I shake my head. "You have to close your office because of me."

I think I'm past tears now, though, to be honest, I'm not sad. I'm weary. I'm looking at the mountain ahead of me, and even though I have no strength left to climb it, I know I have to. I don't have any other option. I'm just sorry that I had to drag anyone else down with me.

He stares at me as though I've just offered to climb a pole and give lap dances to every biker in the club. "You don't have to do anything, Annie," he says slowly. "You didn't bring any of this on yourself. You sure as hell didn't expose me to this weirdo letter-writer. I have to protect myself, and there's no way I'm going to leave you now, whether you can pay me as your investigator or not." He kneels on the office carpet and looks like he wants to touch me, take my hand, but he doesn't. He stands back up and shoves his hands deep into his pockets. "I promised to keep you safe. There's no price tag on that promise, babe."

Suddenly, the tension between Josh and me is as hot as the Florida sunshine. I don't know what I said or what's changing between us, but it suddenly hits me that we're going to be holed up together, I bark out a nervous laugh.

"I guess it's a good thing we're pretending to be together," I say, my voice shaking slightly. "I don't know who Crow is, but I'm grateful he won't be needing his room for a while."

Josh licks his lips, and all I can feel is the throb of heat between my legs. "Let's do this," he says, turning suddenly and heading into his office. "I need to make a sign for the door, grab my shit. You need to put everything you brought from the hotel and everything in your trunk into my truck."

He's all business again, and I wish we could have spent a few more minutes in that sexy, sweet space. Where I could indulge in the fantasy that Josh is mine and that he really will protect me because he wants to, not because I hired him.

"Did you check out of the hotel?" he asks as he rummages through the drawers of his desk.

"Yeah, but only after I cleared out the minibar and trashed the room. I hope you don't mind."

He has his laptop in his hands, and he freezes, looks at me, and then shakes his head. A low rumble of a laugh slips from between his lips.

"Annie Hancock," he breathes. "You're something else."

He unplugs the coffeemaker, tapes a handwritten

sign facing outward on the door, then puts a hand on the small of my back.

"You ready?" he asks. "Make sure you grab your parking pass from your car."

I nod, the reality slowly hitting me. "I'm going to have to talk to my dad, aren't I?"

He locks his inner office and slings a dark-brown leather messenger bag over his chest. "We can talk about it. I think we'll have lots of time to talk about what comes next."

I watch as he turns out the lights and locks up his office. I can see Alice standing in the office next door. She and Morris are kissing, and he's got his hands on her ass. The level of grope that's going on makes me feel a little guilty. I shouldn't be watching Morris grind on his pretty wife, and yet I don't want to look away. That is what real love looks like.

Marriage, children, a biker, and his babe.

I've never seen that kind of love before, and hell, I've certainly never seen that kind of lust. It's more than just sweet. It fills me with a longing so powerful, I'm not sure if I should laugh or cry.

To be loved so deeply and so openly. To have someone I belong to so completely. It's something I want as much as I want to find myself as an artist.

I don't think I realized until now that what Morris and Alice have is possible. It's certainly nothing I ever saw between my parents. I was way too young when Mom died to have even a single memory of what they were like as a couple.

And I've never felt anything like that for any of the guys I've dated or slept with.

I nudge Josh in the ribs.

"What?" he asks.

I motion toward the office. "If that's what big, bad bikers are like, I think I'm going to enjoy living at the compound."

Josh raises a brow at me after seeing the way Morris is manhandling his wife. "If that's what you're into, babe, you just say the word. But you say it to me, got it?"

My cheeks flush so hot, I'm tempted to fan myself. I meet Josh's eyes, and he gives me a look that just does me in.

It's official.

I'm crushing hard on my PI.

———

By the time we pull into the motorcycle club compound, the sun is setting, and I'm starving, exhausted, and angry. Josh and I went to the police department to file a report about the letters and the trashed dorm room. The result was exactly what I expected—there was no crime being committed. No evidence that I was being tracked without my consent since I couldn't locate a tracker on my car.

The officer who took the report was professional and pleasant, but realistic. She gave me a pamphlet about stalking and explained that if there was a demand for money or any damage to property that was not on the school's campus, I should call them or come back in.

Josh didn't seem as discouraged as I was. He lifted the sunglasses off his face and turned to face me. "You want to settle in?" he asks. "Unload the truck then grab some dinner? Carnival Pizza or County Fair Burgers?"

I look at him, confused, but then start cracking up. "There's no such thing as Carnival Pizza or County Fair Burgers. Don't you make promises you can't keep."

His grin is sexy and sweet as he shakes his head. "Come on, Annie. Time to meet the bikers."

The compound itself is surprisingly normal. Lots of motorcycles are parked outside, and when we knock, the door is opened by a woman with loads of wrinkles and even more sass.

"Arrow, you sonofabitch," she says, putting a hand on her hip. "If I'da known you had an old lady, I wouldn't have tried to seduce you so many times."

My mouth falls open.

The woman laughs and laughs until a fit of very raspy coughs replaces the giggles. "I'm shitting you," she says, opening the door wide. "Come on in. Morris told me to expect you."

"I'm Annie," I say as we walk inside.

"Well, aren't you a sweet little thing. Midge, babe. I'm basically the heart and soul of this group of hellions." The woman has a lit cigarette pinched between two fingers, which she waves in the air for emphasis.

"Don't believe a thing she says." An enormous man with dark hair, dark eyes, and a serious set of biceps nods at us. "Arrow," he says. "Good to see you, man. This your old lady?"

Josh claps the man in a half hug, then turns to me. "Annie, this is Logan, but you can call him Crow."

"Pleasure, Annie." Crow holds out his hand to me, and I shake it, trying not to giggle. This man looks like every stereotype and then some. But his hand is firm, his handshake gentle. And I notice a tattoo on his finger where a wedding band would go.

"Nice to meet you," I say. "Is it your room that we're taking?"

Crow nods. "I'm not here much anymore. Wife wouldn't love it if I spent too many nights with these bozos." He gestures to an unbelievably huge man who's lumbering past, an empty plastic drinking cup that probably holds a liter of liquid in it in his hand.

"Fuckin' running a women's shelter now," I hear him grumble as though he's talking to us.

Crow hooks a thumb over his shoulder. "Don't worry about Tiny," he says. "He's one of the last bachelors left. He misses the good old days when the Disciples..." Crow shoots a look at Josh. "Let's just say Tiny's stuck in the past."

"Fuck off, Crow!" Tiny's shout echoes through the compound. "Domesticated motherfuck..."

I look at Josh nervously. "Are you sure this is okay?" I ask quietly. "I don't want to put anyone out..."

Crow holds up a finger and stops my question. "Tiny!" he yells. "Come meet Annie, Josh's old lady." Crow turns and heads toward a large, modern-looking kitchen. Tiny has one side of the refrigerator open, and he's dumping a mountain of ice into his cup.

"Why do they keep calling me an old lady?" I whisper to Josh. "I'm in my twenties, for crap's sake."

"It has nothing to do with age," he whispers back. "I'll explain later."

Midge is in the kitchen too, tearing open a bag of potato chips.

"How's work?" Josh asks Crow, ignoring Tiny and Midge...and me.

"It's good," he says, nodding. "We have our slow seasons, but this summer was the tits. I'm looking to hire more guys on my crew. Flooring subs, electrical, plumbing. Birdie's running the office now, handling the certs and shit from all the subcontractors. It's a goddamn full-time job making sure everyone from demo to finish carpentry's got insurance."

I know a thing or two about construction from working with my dad, so I follow along mostly with what they're saying.

"You kids staying for dinner?" Midge asks, stuffing a handful of chips into her mouth.

I look to Josh, who shakes his head. "We've got plans, thanks. I thought we'd unload the truck before it gets too late."

"I'm out of here." Crow taps his fingers on the counter and wishes everyone a good night. "See you in the morning, man," he calls to Tiny. "I got to be on the job by seven tomorrow."

"Go straight there," Tiny grunts with a wave of his hand. "I'll meet you. Kiss Birdie for me."

Crow claps a hand on Josh's back and wishes me good night.

"Nice to meet you, Crow," I say.

Then, Tiny turns and glares at Josh. "You," he says. "In my office."

Josh nods, and we follow Tiny down along a hallway to an office. For a minute, I feel like I am on the set of a TV show, and it's unlike any room I've ever been in.

Tiny has an extra-large desk and an office chair to match, but it still squeaks under his weight when he sits. He points to two wooden chairs opposite his, and like we're interns interviewing for a position with the CEO, Josh and I look at each other, then cautiously take a seat.

"So," Tiny says, "I hear you got trouble?"

Josh nods. "It happens, man. We could use a place to crash until I sort shit out."

Tiny looks at me, his lips firm but his eyes soft. "And you…Annie, is it?"

I nod. "Annie Hancock, sir."

Tiny laughs so hard, he almost spits out a mouthful of soda. "Sweetheart, you can call me Tiny. Now." He opens a desk drawer and pulls out two sets of keys. "This is what you need to know." He slides one small ring with two keys on it toward me and another toward Josh. "The silver key will let you into the front door of the compound," he says. "The gold key locks your room."

I hold the keys in my hand, but I never take my eyes off the massive biker.

"This is normally something we do not do." He punctuates each word to let me know exactly how he feels about this situation. But then a beat-up-looking cell phone vibrates on the desk. "Excuse me a minute," he says. "Marla?" he says, swiping to unlock the phone. "I'm with some people. Can I call you right back?" He hangs up the phone.

Josh grins but doesn't say anything.

Tiny shoots him a look. "As I was saying. We don't normally let outsiders into this space. This place is sacred. We're more than just a brotherhood. We're a family. Tighter than tight. Closer than blood." He points a thick finger at Josh. "Not that long ago, this son of a bitch helped my daughter and our brother Leo out of a jam. Which makes you one of us. Your enemy," Tiny says, his voice deadly serious, "is my enemy."

He takes a break to sip his drink and wipe his forehead with the back of his hand. "So, for as long as you need a place, you're welcome. I'm going to bitch and moan from time to time, but that's my way. I'm old-school. Bikers had bitches, and compounds weren't for kids and fucking families."

He turns one of the pictures around, and I see a family portrait of a girl who I assume is Tiny's daughter. She's clutching a newborn baby, and a really handsome guy in a leather vest is kissing her head. Tiny glowers behind them, looking somehow angry and proud all at once. "I got a fucking family now, so I guess it comes for all of us eventually." He chuckles. "So, welcome home. Midge will show you where the laundry is and which room is yours. Eat, drink, shower, fuck—the place is your home as long as you want it. And if you know more about this threat you're facing, Arrow, your job is to tell me everything. A threat to one of us is a threat to all of us. We clear?"

Josh is agreeing with Tiny and thanking him, but all I can hear is the echo of one word—fuck.

I may be safe, but I feel like my time here is going to cause a whole lot of trouble.

CHAPTER 10
ARROW

"I'VE BEEN MEANING to ask, why do they call you Arrow?"

Annie and I are eating burgers and fries in the bed of my truck, watching the sun set over the compound. I don't think I've ever had a more romantic night, which says a lot about my recent dating life.

I grin as I dip my burger in a little to-go cup of ketchup. "Aronowicz is a fucking mouthful," I tell her. "And when all my friends were getting into drugs and petty criminal shit, taking on street names like Cobra and Slash, the last thing I wanted was to be called Josh." I chuckle. "It was kind of a play on words. Straight as an arrow. I hung with some rough kids, but I kept my nose clean."

"Is that how you ended up a PI?" Annie's sitting cross-legged, her maxi dress tucked around her knees. Her hair is loose, and the rosy-gold light of the setting sun lights up her eyes and smile. She's fucking gorgeous even with a mouthful of hand-cut fries and a smudge of mustard on the corner of her mouth. She licks it away and then continues, "Hanging with the bad kids?"

"Pretty much. I wasn't involved in their shit, but I was no rat. I ended up being the kid everybody else called when they got wasted and were stuck someplace. I think I bailed out my first buddy before I could even drive."

Annie frowns at that. "What about your parents?" she asks. "How did you have money for bail?"

I suck in a breath through my nose and sigh. "I had a shit family," I admit. "No other way to slice it. I had an old man who left after I was born, and Mom was…" I shrug. "Short version is I grew up fast. I was working for cash in local diners, doing dishes and hauling boxes. Anything anybody would pay me to do, I did. I met a lot of shitheads doing work like that. I knew I couldn't get into trouble. I was one wrong look away from my ma kicking my ass to the curb or getting myself thrown in a group home." I pause to take a sip of my Coke and another bite of my burger.

Annie's face looks troubled, and she shifts her weight a little like she's trying to get comfortable, but she ends up scooting a little closer to me.

"So that's that," I say. "I've pretty much raised myself since I was twelve. I kept out of trouble, saved my money, and ran with a crowd of people who were in similar circumstances. When the time came to move out of my ma's house, I knew there was no college in my future. And I didn't have white-collar aspirations. I like being out on the streets, doing shit. Making things happen."

"But, Josh," she says, sounding sad. "What about, like, holidays, love, and family? Did you have girl-friends who took you in?"

I nod. "Sometimes, yeah. And don't get me wrong. I have friends. I just spent a lot of time around people who had lives as rough or even worse than I had it. When we all got older and guys I'd known since I was fourteen got busted for harder shit, real crimes, I looked into how to make a living doing what I was basically already doing for free." I polish off my meal and stuff my trash in the takeout bag. "Thought about becoming a lawyer for a while," I admit, surprised that I am sharing this with her. I lower my voice, a weird mix of embarrassment and pride tightening my gut. "That's something I've never told anyone before."

"Yeah?" She's stopped eating, holding the burger in her hand and her eyes wide. "What stopped you?"

I rub my fingers together in the universal sign for money. "I had no way to pay for college, so making it all the way through law school seemed impossible. I didn't want to be a cop," I say. "No disrespect to the boys in blue, but…" I shrug. "I never wanted to cuff the bad guys. I could relate to them, and I thought I'd be helping if I made it possible for them to get another chance."

She swallows, and I watch the long column of her pretty throat as the last shadows darken into night around us.

"For a while, I was a bond agent. Making sure guys

showed up to their court appearances, fulfilled their duty. It was a way I could use the trust I had from guys like me who'd gone the wrong way to help them either stay out of prison, or, if that was what was in the cards, I made sure they didn't become fugitives. But that's rough work, and the pay—" I don't really want to go into the subject of money at the moment, considering the fact that I'm hurting for it and Annie doesn't exactly have a trust fund either. "So, I moved into PI work a year ago. I chase a lot of cheating spouses and insurance fraud cases, but it's a living."

She looks troubled, and I want to kiss the frown that pulls on her lips. "What's your dream, Josh? If you could do anything, education and money not being in the way, what would you do?"

That's a question I haven't thought about for a long, long time. I take a minute to really consider it.

"I want a family," I tell her. "You know when those guys were calling you old lady? That's what the bikers call their wives. Their bitches, their old ladies, their women. Talk like that doesn't fly in every circle, but here?" I motion toward the compound, now bathed in darkness. A few lights reflect in the windows, but most of the building is dark. "I'd like that. Guys who are like brothers to me. Guys who I can call in good times. Not just in bad. An old lady to come home to. I don't really give a shit what I do for work. I work hard, and I want to make money and support myself. I never want to lean on anybody else. But how I earn it?" I shrug. "I could be a butcher, a baker, a candlestick maker. I don't give a fuck. It's what I come home to after doing that shit all day that matters."

Annie is quiet. Not chewing, not smiling. Just thinking.

"Thank you for being honest," she says. "I'm glad to know the real you. Not just the answers you think a client would want to hear."

"You're not exactly a client, babe," I say, trying to lighten the mood. "And all that shit I said doesn't mean I won't tear a new asshole in the fucknut who's been sending these letters when we find out who's doing this. Just because I said I don't care what I do doesn't mean I don't care about the work I am doing."

"Oh no, I get that." Annie quietly rolls her trash into a ball and tucks it neatly into the carryout bag. "And thank you. I don't know what I would be doing right now without you."

I reach out my hand and snag her trash, then step onto the bumper and over the side of the truck. I take her hand and help her over the side, then lace my fingers through hers. "Is now a good time to tell me about your dad?" I ask. "Why won't you go home, Annie?"

She sighs as we head toward the compound hand in hand. It doesn't feel like an act. It feels so natural. Like this is how it always has been. Always will be. It's a feeling that I don't want to end.

"Well, like I told you, Dad's been struggling over the last year. I thought maybe he was hiding a health issue or something. He broke up with Cathy. Started spending a lot more time at the office. Just generally seemed different, if you know what I mean. And then this summer, things got really weird. He sent me off to school on short notice. Basically, he pushed me out of working for him."

She swings our hands lightly and I have to tuck the trash under my arm so I can dig in my pocket for the keys to the compound. There's no way I'm letting her go.

"It may sound weird, but I feel like Dad has something big going on, and I guess maybe I'm afraid," she admits. "If Dad has cancer or something really serious, God, I just… I'm only twenty-five, Josh. I lost my mom so young. I'm not ready to face losing him. I want to be there for him, of course, but he doesn't want that right now. He's made it clear he wants some distance, if anything. Maybe he's trying to get me ready for the day he won't be here. Giving me a chance to figure out my life and my art. So that when the day comes that I wake up and I'm all alone in this world, I didn't waste the opportunities he gave me. Even if part of the cost for that means us spending a little less time together."

I unlock the door, let Annie through, then lock the dead bolt behind us. Finding the trashcan in the kitchen, I ditch our carryout, then turn to face her.

"You'll never be alone, Annie." It's not a vow or a promise. It's a fact. "You're beautiful and so damn sweet. You're light, pure light. Maybe your father knows he can't be everything you need in your life. Maybe he wants to give you time to shine."

She nods, but she looks so lost and sad, I want to lift her face and kiss her until she feels nothing but bliss. Nothing but me.

But that's not cool. I don't know how far I think I can take this fake-dating situation, but I'd better put some distance between us because I'm in danger with Annie Hancock. I'm in danger of falling.

"Think the showers are gross?" she asks, a small smile on her face. "I'd love to clean up before bed."

"I think we should find out," I say.

We head toward our room, where we unpacked our clothes before we ran out for those burgers. The compound is quiet tonight. I can hear a TV in the distance, Tiny's voice, and a couple of the other guys cheering over a game. It's homey here in a way that surprises me. I can see why my buddy Leo, Tiny's son-in-law, decided to prospect into the Disciples. They stopped being a gang, running on the wrong side of the law, not too long ago. Now, it's really a club here. A home and family. Who knows. Maybe when all this shit blows over, I'll learn to ride.

Belonging someplace has to start with people you want to belong with. And Annie's making me see all kinds of possibilities.

———

My hair is still damp, and I've thrown on a loose tee and some boxer briefs to sleep in. I normally sleep in nothing but the skin I was born in, but I don't think Annie needs to see my business the first night we're sharing the same room.

While I wait for Annie to finish in the shower, I drag an extra blanket from the closet onto the floor and take one of the two pillows from the bed and drop it on the blanket. I stretch out on the floor and check out the small TV Crow's got in his room. It's not huge, but the compound has every possible streaming service, so by the time Annie opens the door, I've got some choices lined up.

"What are thinking, babe?" I call out before she closes the door. "Horror? Thriller? Movie? Show?"

She's clutching a small pink-striped bag in front of her chest. She looks from me to the TV and then back to me. "What's this? What are you doing?" She pads on bare feet over to a dresser and sets her little bag on top. "Josh?" she asks, her voice soft. "Why are you on the floor?"

I sit upright and smooth back my hair. "I want you to be comfortable," I say. "Did you expect something different?"

She gives me an uncertain smile, and for the first time, I notice what she's wearing. The most freaking adorable button-down top. It's turquoise blue and has pink and orange cupcakes on it, but the thing I love the most is how thin the fabric is. I can make out the hard tips of her nipples through the cotton. And her sleep shorts... Fuck, they give new meaning to the word short. They barely cover anything, and if she turns, which I am begging the angels in the sky above that she will, I'll get more than an eyeful of Annie's delicious ass.

"I thought we'd share this," she says, motioning toward the bed. "It's big enough, and I don't snore."

My cock stiffens at the thought of sleeping

anywhere close to Annie. Her long, smooth legs under the sheets. That perfect ass just inches away from my hands. I don't know if this is such a good idea. I mean, it's a fucking great idea. I want nothing more from life right now than to slide into bed beside Annie Hancock. But whether I can stop myself from treating her like she really is mine… That's something I can't promise.

"Are you sure?" I ask, my voice nearly cracking. "You're all right with this?"

"I'll feel safer," she says, not a single note of doubt in her voice. "Please?"

She doesn't have to ask me twice. I grab the pillow from the floor and toss it back onto the bed. Then I pick up the blanket and drape it at the foot. "Lady's choice," I say, tugging back the sheet and the light quilt on the bed. "Which side?"

"Underneath you?" she says, meeting my eyes.

A bolt of heat hits my cock at her words, and I groan. "Annie," I breathe.

"I want you to hold me," she says. "Will you do that?"

Ah. Okay. I got it. She wants the closeness and the safety. While all I can think about is stripping off those shorts and bouncing my hand off her tight ass until she's dripping, begging me for more, she wants the teddy bear. When it comes to Annie, I will take what I can get.

"Yeah," I grunt, hoping against fucking hope that I can get under the covers before my raging boner gives her a reason to change her mind. "Come here, baby."

She flips off the light switch by the door and turns

the lock before she climbs into bed beside me. I lift my arm, and she nestles against my chest. I point the clicker at the TV and hope my dick won't tent the goddamn sheets. Or if it does, at least I hope she won't notice.

"This one?" I whisper, my voice thick. I can smell the sweetness radiating off her skin. Whether it's lotion or soap or, God, just her, I'm going nuts trying to keep my hands to myself. I grip the remote and stare straight ahead. "Or this?"

I'm flipping channels like it's my job when Annie sighs and rests a hand on my belly. "You pick," she says. "I'm so wiped, I just want to listen and not think."

She's tired, not horny.

Not attracted to me.

That's all right. I can fucking take this. I pick an action movie that I've seen before. Something with a lot of flashing lights, blood, and very little plot. I give the movie a sliver of my attention, but it's something to stare at while I try to ignore the gentle movements of Annie's body against mine. Her long hair is damp and soft, and I can't fucking help myself. While her face is against my chest, I stroke my fingers across her forehead, push her hair back, and gently massage the back of her neck.

"Ooh," she moans. "Ohh, that's nice." She lightly strokes my chest with her fingers while I knead her tight muscles. "I can't believe it's only been two days," she says. "I feel like I've known you forever."

I know the feeling. But I can't say anything. I don't know what to say. I don't care if I've known her two days, two hours, or two years. Annie is everything I'm into. And I want so badly to be inside her.

"Josh?" She suddenly sits up, cocking her head to the side. "Would you do something for me?"

I bark a laugh. "Yeah, babe. I'll do whatever you want." Except move the goddamn sheet from my lap.

She kneels on the bed facing me, her eyes excited. "Your tattoos. I want to see all of them."

Oh fuck.

"I've got 'em everywhere, Annie. Back, arms, and…"

"And?" She grins, her brows lifting.

I shake my head. "Annie, I did some stupid shit when I was younger. Nothing illegal, right? But…"

"Is your penis tattooed?" she asks, but she doesn't sound scandalized.

Right now, I wish my dick had ink because I would love nothing more than to show it to her. But no, my dick is just the way I was born with it. "No," I say, "but my ass cheeks are."

She claps her hands and practically bounces on the bed. "I need to see," she begs. "Seriously, you can't tell me your ass is tattooed and then not show me."

"I can't just show you my ass, Annie." I shake my head. "Seriously, I've got some major low-class ink back there, babe. I just…"

But then she moves her fingers to the top button of her pajama top. She slowly unbuttons just the first one. "I'll show you mine if you show me yours," she says.

"You have a tattoo?"

A deep pink flush covers her cheeks. "I want to see your ass, Josh."

"All right. First, top half." I work my arms through the sleeves of my tee and toss the fabric onto the floor. She leans close and inspects my ink.

"Tasteful," she says, nodding, the long strands of her hair covering her nipples. "Sexy, even."

I have to bite back a smile. "You think I'm sexy." It's more of a statement than a question as I rake a hand through my hair. "Well, this is going to change your mind fast."

She claps her hands as I climb off the bed. "Show me your booty," she chants again.

I start cracking up as I slip my fingertips under the waistband of my briefs and face the wall. "Now, you promised," I remind her, "if I show you mine, you'll show me yours."

"Oh yeah," she says, giggling. "A deal's a deal."

I tug the right side of my briefs down, sighing dramatically. Normally the first time a woman sees my ass is after we've been intimate. By then, I'm past the worry that my tattoo is going to be the reason she doesn't let me into her pants.

But if Annie's going to show me hers, I'm biting the bullet. I shove down just enough of my briefs to reveal my entire right cheek.

"Whoa," she gasps. I hear her move across the bed, and then I feel the gentle pressure of her fingertips lightly tracing the design.

Fuck me.

I grit my teeth together to hold back a groan as the blood fires through my cock like a freaking cannon.

She's exploring the wildly colorful design in silence until she finally asks, "So, I can tell it's a crown..." She sounds apologetic.

"It's all right," I say, "I know it's the most shit-looking crown ever." I mean, Jesus. I'm showing this thing to an actual artist. I tug the fabric back over my ass and give my dick a minute to cool itself down before turning back to her and climbing back in bed.

Her giggle is back. "What exactly does it mean?"

I yank back the blanket and slide into bed, hopefully before she sees I've got an erection as tall as Tiny is wide.

"My buddy Anthony thought it was clever. He was practicing with his first gun. I was his first human canvas."

"Josh..." Her fingers touch the space over my heart, stroking the light hairs that dust my still-bare chest. "Why the crown?"

I groan and close my eyes, dropping my head back against the wall behind the bed. "That I'm an ass king," I blurt out. "I've always had a thing for a great behind."

Annie is silent for a second, and then she laughs so hard and so long, I can't help but laugh with her. Once she's breathing normally and she's stopped shaking her head, I grow serious.

"So," I remind her, my eyes narrowing. "I believe it's your turn, babe."

She nods and then licks her parted lips. "Well," she says, "I..." Her hands are on the second button of that cupcake shirt. If she doesn't hurry up and open it, I'm going to eat my way through and not stop until I feel her hot skin between my teeth.

"Annie?" I urge.

"I didn't realize you were a butt guy," she says, a sudden shyness flushing her cheeks. "I assumed most guys like boobs."

"Ass king is just my tattoo, but I love it all," I assure her.

I'm curious what an artist would value so much that she'd permanently ink the symbol or the object into her skin. I can't even guess what it will be. Something girly or artistic…maybe pretty words.

My fingertips are burning to touch her as her fingers find the last button on her cupcake top. The sides fall open, leaving the middle of her body partially exposed, revealing just the sexiest bit of cleavage and a soft, smooth stomach.

God, I am dying to see her. All of her.

Now that we're alone in this bed, all I can think about is bending her legs and touching her pussy. I want to look at every inch of her, taste her skin, and fuck her until she's screaming for release.

And that ass.

I want to bend her over my lap and spank those tight cheeks until her juices run down her thighs. I want to see how many times I can make her come with my fingers before I claim her with my cock.

I try to break up my frantic thoughts, my desperate desire for this woman, by reminding myself this is just a game. None of this is real. But then, Annie works the cupcake top over her shoulders and lets it drop to the bed.

She kneels before me, her tits bare, with her lips slightly parted.

"Annie," I whisper, my eyes caressing the tight globes of her breasts. They are smaller than I imagined but even more spectacular.

My breathing is ragged, and my dick is so hard, I'm sure the tip is weeping a river into my briefs.

"Annie," I rasp, clenching my hands into fists under the blanket. "I don't see a tattoo."

"Josh…" Her gaze never leaves mine. "I don't have any tattoos."

CHAPTER 11
ANNIE

I'M LITERALLY KNEELING topless in front of a man I hardly know in a strange bed, but somehow, I've never wanted anything more in my life. All the anxiety about my art, the letters, my father… It all fades away as I watch Josh's jaw clench.

"I, uh, never actually said I had a tattoo," I whisper, suddenly feeling a little nervous. Maybe I'm stupid for feeling this way, but Josh is sweet, gorgeous, and damn if he doesn't make me forget everything about the world that scares me. "I hope that's…"

I can't finish the sentence because he leans forward, reaches a hand behind my hair, and gently draws my face close to his. "Annie," he breathes, a sweet puff of breath teasing my lips. "Is this what you want?"

My eyes flutter closed and a half moan slips from between my lips. I feel the throb between my legs intensify, and I know it makes no sense.

I want this. I want him.

I can't speak.

I open my eyes and look into his, his gaze searing hot. His nostrils flare, and he waits. Waits for me to say or do something. To confirm that no matter how many hours we've known each other, that this is more than okay.

"Please, Josh," I whisper, closing my eyes. "I want you."

I've hardly said the words when I feel his lips against mine. His trim beard scratches my chin, and all I can think is how good that's going to feel all over my body. With the first press of his tongue against my mouth, I open to him. If I'd thought Josh was hot before, tasting him flips my freaking world upside down.

The kiss starts sweet and slow. He tastes and explores my lips, his tongue dancing against mine. But then his fingers tighten in my hair and he's moving onto his knees to bring me closer. I'm breathless, lost to the feeling of his mouth against mine. He tastes so sweet.

I rake my hands up the muscles of his bare back and moan into his mouth. "You feel so good," I pant. "Josh, my God…"

"Baby," he grunts, hardly able to pull his mouth from mine. "I want to do every dirty thing to you and more, but I didn't think to pack any condoms."

I lean away from him slightly and pout. "Do everything else, then," I say. "We'll have an excuse to take it slow. I mean, slower."

He nods and cups the back of my neck, then stares into my eyes. "You're fucking unreal," he says, his voice soft. "You're…" He trails off, and I cock my chin at him.

"I'm wearing too many clothes," I complain, giving him a smirk.

"I'll handle that," he says.

My breasts are aching. I mean, I feel every beat of my heart pulsing at my nipples. I am dying to feel his touch, but Josh turns his attention to my pajama bottoms. He works the loose elastic over my hips and lowers the cupcake shorts to the bed.

I put a hand on his shoulder and lift one leg so he can work the shorts over my thigh and down around my ankle, then he does that with the other leg, until finally, I'm bare before him.

He's still wearing his boxer briefs, and I'm freaking thrilled to see it. The front of his shorts reveals he's as excited as I am, and I am immediately seriously rethinking my stance on safe sex.

A sudden shyness overtakes me, but Josh takes charge.

He grabs a pillow and sets it halfway down the length of the bed. "Lie down on your belly," he orders.

I cover my mouth, hiding my amusement. "Ass king," I whisper.

He's shaking his head, but his grin is as big as mine as I settle on the bed. I prop the pillow beneath my stomach and rest my face to the side.

"Anything off-limits?" he asks, and I feel his large, warm hands on my calves. He's caressing the muscles, but I'm so soft and relaxed under his attention, I couldn't care less about anything else in the world.

"No," I say, deciding to trust him completely. "Just please don't stop."

The movie on the TV shifts into a really bright action sequence, and I close my eyes and focus only on Josh's touch.

He nudges my legs apart a bit, helping me spread open a little wider until I feel his fingers between my thighs. "How's this?" he asks, his voice sounding as thick and raw as I feel.

My blood is sluggish, my eyes sealed shut, and I'm locked away in the happiest place I can ever remember being. Josh rubs my inner thighs with a motion that's deep and sensual.

"Fucking amazing," I pant, unable to open my eyes.

It feels too good. He feels too good.

I just want to stay here, my skin under his hands, for days.

I let a little moan slip out when I feel his hot breath against my butt cheek. He's kissing the side of my behind, one hand caressing the curve where my butt and leg meet.

"Josh," I whimper as my legs start to tremble. "That's so fucking good."

He works his fingers higher, stroking my cheeks and blowing hot kisses against my skin. "How do you feel about a little pressure?" he asks. "Like this. Too much?"

I feel the cool air against my skin as he moves his hand from the back of my thigh, and a moment later, he brings his palm against me in a firm, but not hard, spank.

I suck in a lungful of air in surprise and shock. He spanked me. No one has ever done that to me before, and I cannot believe how fucking good it feels. The way he did it, there was no loud slapping sound, no pain, just a delicious pressure with a little more sharpness to it. The contact makes my legs feel weak, and my pussy becomes wetter.

I'm into it. It feels good. Like I want it again good.

"More," I whisper, arching my hips to lift my ass cheeks closer to him.

"Just relax, babe." He runs a hand along my lower back and coaxes me to lie flat. Then, just as I'm wiggling my toes and comfortable, there it comes again.

Spank.

"Fuck, Josh." That one was harder, a decisive smacking sound echoing over the noise of the movie. Pleasure floods my limbs, and I groan as he kisses the area he just touched. I feel the heat of his breaths, the softness of his lips, and then, Oh, sweet God, I feel the prickles of his beard as he rubs his face against my cheeks.

I spread my legs wider and start to rock my hips, desperate to relieve the ache of need.

"What turns you on, babe?" he rasps against my skin. He's stroking me now, running his fingertips from the backs of my thighs to my lower back, trailing along my ass crack as he moves.

I grunt against the sheets, and Josh laughs softly.

"Say again, baby? I didn't get that."

I turn my face away from the mattress and lick my lips. "Everything," I tell him. "Everything you do."

"Good," he says. "Now, turn over. I want to watch your gorgeous face as I make you come."

The breath catches in my chest, but I obey, willing my pleasure-drenched legs to move so I can roll onto my back. I smooth the hair back from my face, and Josh moves the pillow that was under my belly to under my ass.

"Your fucking tits," he says, shaking his head. "Sensitive?"

I nod. "I'm dying over here," I admit. "Your beard on my nipples could probably make me come."

"Probably?" he echoes. "Sounds like a challenge, Annie."

I swallow and wonder just what I've gotten myself into. A sexy man I've only just met, and here I am telling him my body's deepest secrets. And worse, I'm handing him the keys to the most intimate parts of myself, and it feels so damn right.

I throw my head back against the pillows and spread my legs open. "That was more than a challenge. It was an invitation. Please, Arrow. I need you to make me come."

His eyes flash dark before I close mine and see nothing but darkness. I want to watch him, to see that beautiful mouth claim my tits, but the moment he strokes his chin across my nipple, I cry out and grab his hair.

"Too much?" he asks, but I can't answer.

I grunt some animal sound that is supposed to sound like no and pull his face closer to my chest.

He chuckles, which I assume means he gets the message, and then flicks the tip of his tongue against the tip of my nipple.

I've always had super-sensitive nipples, but in Josh's mouth, it's as if a live electrical wire is connecting my breasts and my pussy. He works my tip between his lips, sucking and licking and nipping it between his teeth until I'm so aroused, I'm literally writhing beneath him on the bed.

"Fuck," he says, murmuring the words against my raw skin. "The way you move."

"Don't stop," I plead.

He chuckles deep in his chest, and I feel the weight of his body pressing against mine as he clamps a nipple between his teeth and tugs. "I won't, baby. I won't."

Before I can explode from the pressure of his mouth on my tits, he pulls away and situates himself between my legs. I don't wait to be told what he wants. I spread my legs open and peek through my lids as he looks at my pussy. The dark-blond hair is trimmed, and he works his fingers through it to find my drenched folds.

I gasp and nearly cry out when I feel him stroke my outer lips.

Fuck, this man knows his way around a woman's body. He gently taps my wetness with his fingertips, then rubs the dampness into my outer lips. His touch is light, and my clit is on fire. Throbbing with yearning for his strong, confident hands to take me past the point of no return.

"I'm going to go inside you," he says, but he didn't need to warn me. I've wanted this since he flashed me that ass cheek with the crown tattoo on it.

I whimper and buck my hips at the promise of feeling him inside me. "Please," I cry, tensing my thighs.

I feel his thumb press lightly on my clit while he slips two fingers just a tiny bit inside me, then he pulls out.

"Josh!" I cry, my body so close to the release it craves when he takes it all away.

"Let me do this for you, baby," he coaxes, again working his thumb against my clit while he slides two fingertips partway inside me.

I'm gripping the sheets now, silently giving over to his attention. The way he slides in, just a little, just a tease, and then out, the pressure he puts on my clit… I won't even need him all the way inside to explode if he keeps this up.

I can't say anything. Can't cry, can't beg. I'm lost. Lost to the sensation of his fingers on my body, his fingers inside my body, stroking and pressing, sliding and leaving, until, finally, I'm rocking my hips, trying to force his fingers deeper.

He uses one hand to spread my legs, opening me as wide as he can, and just that small movement seems to change the pressure on my clit. The next time he slides inside, he slides deep, crooking his fingers and pressing down on my clit until I explode.

I cry out as I climax, my body spasming against Josh's fingers. Pulse after brilliant pulse rockets through my body, and through the blood raging in my ears, I hear his praise.

"Good girl, come harder. Don't stop."

I don't know if I've come once or twice or if I'm riding an inexhaustible wave of erotic bliss, but it seems like minutes before my pussy stops convulsing. Josh stills his hand, his fingers deep inside me, and drops his head to my belly.

"You're fucking phenomenal," he breathes, planting a kiss in the mist of sweat on my stomach.

"Uh, I'd say you're the phenomenal one." I can hardly form the words, can hardly think, let alone speak. Every inch of my body feels good—better than good…I feel alive.

And what's worse. I'm still hungry for him. For more of this.

I am not going to be able to get enough of Josh. I may not know who I am as an artist or what's going on in my life, but I know this much. I'm falling fast and hard for my PI.

———

Once I get his boxer briefs off, I can't help but take him into my mouth. I feel like I spend an hour with his cock in my mouth, my hands around his shaft, until he finally shudders and rides the waves of pleasure.

The movie is long over, and the TV screen has gone

dark. The logo from the streaming service that we're watching isn't even flashing anymore.

"Josh," I whisper, my eyes so heavy I want to get this out before I crash.

"Mmmm," he hums, and I feel his voice rumble through his chest against my cheek.

"Are we going to make a habit of this?" I ask softly. "Or was this a one-time thing?"

He's really quiet at my question, and I almost regret ruining the moment with a dose of reality. But I'd rather know if he sees this as an isolated hookup.

"I mean," I continue, "I don't want you to feel oblig-ated because we're sharing a bed. Oh fuck, I shouldn't have said anything."

I start to turn over, to curl away from him to give us both some space. This wasn't just sex for me. This was fucking great sex. Connection. Laughter. I know I don't even really know the man, but this feels too right. Like this was meant to be. And if I need to put walls around my heart, I will.

But I need to know sooner rather than later. It would break my heart if the best sex of my life, the most fun I've ever had, was all a lie. Just the ruse of fake dating while we stay in the compound.

"Is that what you want?" he asks. "A one-time thing? Because I'm going to have to sleep on the floor if that's what you want, Annie. I don't think I could stop myself from wanting more of you. All of you. A dozen times a night if I can have you."

I turn back to face him, but I don't cuddle his chest. I hold a light blanket in front of my breasts and stroke the hair away from his forehead. "I want all of you, too," I whisper. "As many times as you'll have me."

He opens his arms, and I finally settle against his chest. A sleepy yawn claims my mouth, and I close my eyes with Josh's arms tight around me. We're naked, wrapped tight together, and in a strange place. But for the first time in forever, I feel like I've come home.

CHAPTER 12
ARROW

FINGER-FUCKING a client may just be the stupidest thing I've done. Ever. And yet, I'm planning on doing it again and again. As many times as she wants.

I wake just after sunrise and check my phone. It's early, but I always rise at this hour and get in a workout before I start the day. I like to give my best energy to the things that matter most to me, and keeping fit has always been a top priority. Whether I need to run from bad guys or chase them down, fitness is practically a requirement of the job.

But now, with Annie asleep beside me, her arm thrown over the sheets and a bare leg sticking out from beneath the covers, I could see a whole new type of priority taking over my mornings.

I slip out of bed, trying to keep from waking her, and slide on my briefs. I grab my keys and hit the bathroom, locking a sleeping Annie inside the room. She'll be able to unlock the door from the inside, but

I'm not taking any chances. I want to have a look around the compound and see if there're any free weights lying around. Worst-case, I can plan for a run tomorrow once I map out a decent route close to the compound.

I hear voices in the kitchen and head that direction. Tiny is sitting on a stool, his elbows leaning against the counter. He's wearing a giant tank top and is panting hard. He's dripping with sweat and cursing.

"Tiny." Even though I'm barefoot and in my underwear, I rush up to him and clap him lightly on the back. "Fuck, man, are you all right?"

He grunts and swats me away with a meaty hand. "Fuck off, Arrow." He shakes his head, and droplets of sweat go flying.

A second later, Leo walks through the front door of the compound, a shit-eating grin on his face. "Arrow, you son of a bitch."

He joins us in the kitchen and gives me a half hug. He's dressed in gym shorts and is shirtless like me.

I jerk a thumb at Tiny. "Everything all right?"

Leo shakes his head. "Now that Tiny has a grand-kid, we're working on a little cardiovascular fitness."

"Fuck that shit." Tiny snorts and rubs his forehead with the back of his palm. "I'm getting guilted into this shit because I have a grandson. What I really care about is getting a little of my mojo back."

"Your mojo back?" Leo asks with a snort.

I grin, remembering that Marla gave Tiny her number. Or vice versa. "You trying to get back into fucking shape, T?" I ask. "No shame in that."

Tiny gives me a blistering glare and hauls himself off the stool. "Don't fucking call me T."

Leo cracks a grin. "He's not a fan of working out. It makes him a little grouchy."

Tiny grunts, pointing a shaking finger at Leo. "We're done. Son-in-law or not, no more working out." He lumbers over to the fridge and yanks it open and curses a blue streak under his breath. "I need a goddamn Coke," he sputters, then heads off toward his office.

Leo shakes his head again, then fires up the coffeemaker. "So, things working out here?" he asks. "Tiny told me you're crashing in Crow's old room with…" Leo gives me a curious look. "Your old lady."

I nod but decide it's better not to get into it. "Yeah, man. Annie and I are really grateful."

He looks like he's about to press me for details, but I don't want to explain. Leo and I are friends, but I've always been tighter with his older brother, Tim. It probably seems a little weird that I've never mentioned Annie before now, but now is definitely not the time either.

Right on cue, Annie rushes into the kitchen, clutching her phone in her hands and looking like she just woke up. Her hair is loose and messy, and she's wearing the same cupcake pajamas from last night. She's biting her lower lip and looking like she's about to break into a run.

Immediately, my body remembers the feel of her ass against my hands and the taste of her nipples in my mouth, but my protective instincts go into overdrive at the raw fear on her face.

"Annie, what is it? What's wrong?"

I cross the kitchen to meet her, and she looks at me with a wobbly smile.

"Hey." I pull her against my chest and kiss the top of her head, then release her and search her face. "What's up? You were sound asleep just a minute ago."

She nods, then holds out her phone to me. "I woke up when you left, so I grabbed my phone to see if you'd texted where you were going." She looks terrified. "I have six messages, Josh. All from the same person."

I take her phone and scroll the messages. "Neveah?" I ask.

Annie nods.

I read the messages and start to feel pressure building behind my eyes after each one. The first message is friendly, but with each additional message, the tone changes. The voice goes cold and almost authoritative.

The last one has me most concerned.

"She says if you don't come to campus this morning and check in with her, she's going to report you as withdrawn to Student Affairs." I hand the phone back to her. "I've never been to college, but that doesn't sound like her job."

Annie shrugs. "I mean, technically, I'm paying for the program. I'm not on scholarship. I should be able to come and go as I please, but I do think one of the conditions of living in the residence hall is if I plan to be away, I need to formally notify my RA. It's a safety concern, I guess. They need to know where I am if I'm not in my room."

I suck in a chest full of the coffee aroma coming from the very full pot Leo's made. "Let's get showered and dressed. I think our first stop today is your dorm."

Annie nods, and I introduce her to Leo. He offers us coffee and reminds us to help ourselves to food. "I'm out, man. See you at the office later?" Leo looks me over, so I assume he hasn't noticed the sign I put on my door back at the strip mall.

"Not likely," I tell him. "I'll be working off-site until we sort this all out."

Leo nods, waves goodbye to Annie, then heads out.

Once we're alone, Annie and I grab cups of coffee and take them back to our room.

She plops down on the bed and looks wrecked. "What is happening?" she whispers. "Could Neveah have something to do with the letters?"

I can tell from the look on her face that the idea of the people she thought she could trust betraying her is eating her up. I wish I could reassure her. I wish I had the answers, but I don't. I know the disappointment of those closest to you letting you down. Fuck, stabbing you right in the belly. But if that's what Annie's facing, she's not going to face it alone.

I sip my coffee, then set it down on Crow's dresser. I sit beside her on the bed and open my arms. She tucks her head under my chest and hugs me. "You'll get through this," I promise. "You're not alone. We're going to sort out exactly who's behind this and why. We're going to stop it, Annie."

I'm not sure my words bring her any comfort. If the one person she cares about at school is somehow behind all this, she may decide, or be forced, to leave. Derailing her dreams is not something I'm looking forward to doing, but if it comes to that, her life will have to come before her art.

I just hope to high heaven I don't have to be the one to tell her that.

———

Annie and I drive my truck onto campus and park in the student lot. I use her student parking permit and almost hope that some campus security officer checks that the tag matches the plates the permit is registered to. I have very little faith that anything like that will happen.

We first head up to the studio just to check if there are any notes left behind. Thankfully, there are none. And no evidence that anything has been moved or disturbed since we were here last.

Then we head to the dorms. Her room is still as messy as we left it, with only the clothes and toiletries that she took to the compound missing. Here, too, looks unchanged and untouched since yesterday.

"That's a relief," Annie says, her shoulders sagging. "No new bad news to deal with."

"Let's do some cleaning," I tell her. "Let's turn on some music and prop that door open, so that anyone who may be interested will know you're here."

She looks nervous, but she nods before she uses the tip of a sneaker to hold open the door. The windows are closed, and the blinds are drawn, so she lifts them halfway up to let in light. It'll be blazing hot in a couple hours, but by then, we'll have made our appearance and can get out of here.

Annie cues up a playlist on her phone and connects to a small speaker.

I cock my chin at her and grin. "You listen to this?"

The first song is a cover of a retro nineties girl band pop hit. The absolute opposite of what I imagine a textile artist would play, but then, I have no freaking idea what kind of music an artist listens to. There is so much I don't know about Annie and so much more I want to learn.

"It's girl-power music," she explains. "I'm not feeling very connected to strength at the moment." She's stepping over piles of clothes and looking like she has no idea where to begin.

"Hey." I toe off my boots, careful to avoid stepping on her underwear and bras, and pull her to standing. "Come here."

I hold her close, and she presses her ear against my chest.

"Why do you smell so good?" she asks, breathing me in.

I laugh. "I don't know, babe. But you smell good enough to eat."

She looks up at me with a smoldering grin just as there's a loud knock on the door.

"Annie freaking Hannie." Neveah storms through the door and practically yanks Annie out of my arms. She holds her close in a hug and rocks her lightly. "I'm so happy to see you, babe."

Neveah's enthusiasm seems genuine until she gets a look at me. "Oh, hey." She nods, but then she looks away and focuses all her attention on Annie. "Where've you been? You've been getting my messages, right?"

I stand back and let Annie handle the situation, but I'm in full observation mode. I watch every move Neveah makes. I study her clothes, her shoes, her hair. There is something about her that is eerily familiar. I can't shake the feeling that I know her from somewhere. That she's someone I may actually have met before.

Annie is making apologies to Neveah and explaining that she's been staying with me and doing great. She lies, saying she hasn't been checking her phone.

Neveah makes a little, "Uh-huh," noise and waves a hand at me. "Okay, so you run out and find a hot boyfriend. You can't at least let me know, so I don't worry?"

Everything she says is right. She sounds like the perfect friend. Reasonable. Thoughtful. But my instincts are firing hard. There's something about this woman that makes me not trust a word coming out of her mouth.

"You want some help? You know you don't have to clean this up alone." Neveah bends down to pick up a paperback book and sets it on Annie's desk.

"I'm not alone," Annie says quietly. "Josh is helping."

"Right, of course, I know. But, like, doesn't he have a job or something to get off to? I got you. That's literally what they're paying me for."

I can tell that Annie is struggling to manage her friend's attention. I pretend to engross myself in moving the mattress back onto the bed frame, but I'm racking my brain.

"Let me help you," Annie offers, lifting one end of the mattress.

She and I position the mattress back on the frame with ease, and that's when it hits me.

I know this woman, and she is not who she says she is.

All of a sudden, I'm faced with a choice. Do I let on to Neveah what I know—and even worse, do I tell Annie?

I decide playing it cool for a bit is the safest path. I get an idea.

"Babe," I say, lifting my brows at Annie. "Is there a cafeteria or a coffee kiosk nearby? I'll grab us some cleaning fuel."

Annie's lips part and she looks like she's about to ask me to stay, but Neveah talks over her.

"This is a closed campus," she says a little stiffly. "You'd need a student ID or a guest pass if you want to eat in the cafeteria." She gives me a sweet and absolutely fake smile. "But I will treat if you'll make a run for lattes."

I stand and nod. "Love that plan."

I think fast. Neveah is obviously trying to separate me from Annie, and I'm pretty sure there's a good reason.

"I'm going to hit the head before I roll out." I slip

into the bathroom attached to Annie's room and tap out a text message to Annie.

Right after I leave for coffee, I'm going to call you. Answer the call. I'll explain on the phone. Got it?

Then I hit send.

While I wait for her to reply, I flush and run the tap so it sounds like I really did come in here to piss.

My phone vibrates with a response to my text.

Got it.

I leave the bathroom and walk into the room, rubbing my hands together. "Okay, ladies. Lay your coffee orders on me."

Neveah asks me to get her some frothy pink drink with extra ice. I notice that she doesn't, as she promised, grab any cash or offer to pay, but I'm okay fronting this expense. I have a plan, and I need Neveah to trust me.

"You know what I want, babe." Annie lifts up on her toes and kisses my cheek, and I think I fall in love with her a little in that moment.

I have no clue what she wants from the coffee shop, but she's playing up the fact that we're dating for Neveah's benefit. I want to crush her body against me and whisper that I can't wait to give her what she wants…but I'll have plenty of time for that tonight.

"Be back before you can miss me," I promise.

I hope Neveah takes that to mean I won't be long. Anything she has to say to Annie, she'd better say right away.

I head down the hall, the opposite direction from the elevator, and into the stairwell, hoping like hell I get cell reception. I punch Annie's number into my phone and dial. She answers on the second ring.

"Hey, you forget something?" she asks.

"Do not end the call," I tell her, speaking quickly and quietly. "Pretend to hang up, but keep your phone on speaker so I can hear your conversation. Make sure she doesn't see."

Annie doesn't respond to what I'm saying, but instead, she says, "Yeah, honey. Let me ask Neveah." I hear shuffling and then the sound clear as day of Annie asking whether Neveah's hungry for lunch. I immediately mute my phone because it sounds like Annie has already put her phone on speaker.

When she comes back to me, she says, "Thanks, but we're both fine with just the drinks. We can eat lunch later." She pauses only a second and then says, "Okay, babe. See you soon," just like she's saying it in response to something I've said. She's acting out the role to perfection.

Then I hear her say to Neveah, "He's such a sweetheart. Gorgeous and sexy, but thoughtful too."

I shake my head and grin. She knows I'm listening to everything she's saying, and fuck, I'm going to pay those compliments back and then some tonight at the compound. I stay in the stairwell listening, having absolutely no intention of actually leaving for coffee yet. If Neveah is who I think she is, Annie should be safe with her. But I want to understand exactly what she's up to.

"All right," I hear Neveah say. Then I hear movement and the slam of Annie's door. "Time for privacy. We need to talk."

She's not wasting any time.

"Okay…" Annie sounds uncertain, and I wish I could reassure her. Prove to her that, no matter what, I'm here for her. I am not going to let anything happen to her. "What do you want to talk about?"

Neveah doesn't say anything right away, but then she launches in and doesn't hold back. "This hunk you've got glued to you. Tell me the truth. How long have you known him?"

Annie stammers but answers in a way that feels sincere. "I mean…not that long, but long enough to know how I feel. Why?"

When Neveah speaks next, her voice is low, but it's incredibly clear. She must be really close to wherever Annie set the phone. "Babe, do you know what he does for a living? Do you have any idea who he really is?"

Annie stumbles over that. "I mean, I think I know. But why? Why are you being so hard on Josh? What do you know? What's the problem, Neveah? You've been acting really weird."

"He's not someone you can trust, Annie." Neveah's voice is clear, but her tone is really setting my teeth on edge. "Listen to me, babe. He's trouble. And all he's going to do is bring that trouble to your door. This?" I picture her sweeping her hand around the mess in Annie's room. "This is because of him. I'm sure of it."

"Wait, what?" Annie sounds genuinely confused, and my gut clenches at the sound. "What do you mean, this is because of him? Josh couldn't have anything to do with this."

I feel sick at the fact that she thinks I might have had

anything to do with what happened to her room. What's happening in her life.

But I want to know exactly what Neveah thinks. And then she says something that makes my belly turn over. "As long as you're with that man, you're in danger."

CHAPTER 13
ANNIE

I KNOW I shouldn't feel unsafe with my friend, but I do. The way she's looking at me. The way she's so insistent that Josh is a freaking danger. I've known her only a few weeks longer than I've known him, but he's never once made me question his intentions. From the very second I met him, he made it clear that he was looking out for my safety, my budget, and my best interests.

And that was before I practically stripped off my pajamas and threw myself at him.

I study Neveah's face and try to ignore the fact that Josh can hear everything we're saying. "I don't get it," I tell her. "Josh has nothing to do with any of this. Why do you think he does?"

Neveah shakes her head dramatically, her colorful buns falling a little looser over her ears. "Girl, what's this about?" She points to the mess in my room. "People lose their keys all the time. I'd know, I have to help them get their asses back into their rooms." She grimaces as if the mess that is my dorm room is obvious evidence. "I've never seen anything like this." She reaches out and rests a hand on my arm, and for a moment, I see a side of her that drops my defenses. "Annie." Her brows lower, and she sounds concerned. Like she's trying not to scare me off. "Sometimes the people we're attracted to don't treat us well all the time. Most of the time, they are fun and loving, but when they get angry or feel threatened…"

I close my eyes and draw in a breath. God. She really is trying to be a friend. She thinks Josh is violent. That he did this to my room?

I shake my head. "No, no," I say, starting to bite my lower lip. She's got it all wrong, but it's not unreasonable that she would ask. Hell, even suspect it. This is her job. I'm sure she's been trained to see stuff like this. I'm sick at the fact that she's probably seen this and so much worse.

But that's not the situation here. Josh is on my side, and I believe that, no matter what, I can trust him. And I desperately want her to do the same. I'm honestly still wrangling with the worry that I cannot entirely trust Neveah.

"He's not…" I try to explain, but I'm at a loss for words. I feel like the only way to clear Josh's name is to tell Neveah about the notes I've been getting. About what's really been going on. But what's the downside to telling her? Will she go to the campus police? I mean, God. They already know about what happened to my room. Maybe the notes will make them take this more seriously.

At this point, I'm hiding out in a motorcycle club

compound. I've made a police report. I probably should make sure that everyone who might need to know what's happening is in the loop.

I try not to peek at my phone as I grab her hand and give it a squeeze. "I think I understand what you're saying, and I love you for caring. But it's not like that." I get up and pace toward the window, hoping to draw her attention toward me and away from the phone. "Josh had absolutely nothing to do with this. I've started bringing Josh around campus because of a problem I've been having."

She grows immediately serious. She stands, a scowl on her face. "What problem, Annie? What's going on?"

I shrug and explain that I've received some notes that started out weird but ended up threatening. I tell her that Josh is the one who insisted I go to the police. That he's been nothing but the shoulder I can cry on through all this. "And worse," I say, shaking my head, "whoever is doing this seems to know how to get to Josh too. That's why I've been off campus. He and I have been staying together someplace where we'll be safe."

Neveah pinches her eyebrows between two fingers and curses under her breath. She presses me for details about the notes. When did they start? What did they say? Do I still have them? She looks so sincerely distraught, I immediately start to feel relief. She can't have anything to do with the notes. She looks like she's about ready to punch somebody for me, if the speed of her pacing and the rapid-fire questions mean anything.

I don't think she's an actor, and I want to trust that her reaction is sincere.

"Babe," she says, dropping back down onto the floor. She sits cross-legged and sighs. "We need to involve the campus police. You're right that you shouldn't be here if you're in any kind of danger. But I have to report this. No matter who's doing this shit to you, whether it's someone you know or not, we need to make sure security is involved. There are protocols for this."

I sniff hard and lift a brow at her, not even bothering to hold back my sarcasm. "Like the protocols they followed when they made the report about my room?"

She nods. "I know. They don't exactly inspire confidence." She gives me a sad half smile, her pretty lips pressing together. "But Annie, if they know what's going on, they can request support from local law enforcement. There are some good officers on the team. I can put in a request to the Department of Residence Life for more security patrols, anything. Until you know who's doing this and why, anyone could be at risk."

I nod. I know she's right. "Okay," I agree. "So, what do I have to do?"

Neveah stands and points a hand at the mess in the room. "Let me help you. Let me in. I can be a friend to you here, Annie. Not just an RA."

I instinctively grab her in a hug, pushing away the smallest part of me that still wonders if maybe, just maybe, she's somehow in on this. Maybe I'm not seeing everything there is to see. Maybe she's not someone I can trust completely. But Josh will be back soon. And no matter what she says, does, or thinks, I trust him.

God, how I trust him. And I'm more grateful than ever to have him in my corner for as long as he plans to be there.

I release Neveah from the hug just as Josh returns with a cardboard to-go caddy filled with drinks.

"Ohh, sweet salvation." Neveah leaps toward him and picks up her drink from the container. "You're a freaking angel." She takes a long, deep sip and closes her eyes. "Hmm-hmm that hits the freaking spot." She turns to me and points. "You. Talk to your man," she says. "I promised I'd treat. I'm going to grab cash from my room."

I don't really care about Neveah's money, but I'm glad she's giving me a minute alone with Josh. I grab my phone off the floor where I had it facedown so the lock screen wouldn't reveal there was a connected call. I quickly swipe, end the call, and jam the phone into my pocket.

"Hey." I lower my voice and take the drink caddy from him. "You heard all that?"

He nods and pulls me close to him. His arms are hot from the Florida sun, and he holds me tight against his chest. I smell the warm heat of his body, the enticing hint of his cologne.

"You smell good," I mutter, lifting my face to his. "You're seriously distracting, you know that?"

He laughs and plants a light kiss against my lips. "You did good, babe. Really good."

Shivers travel up my arms and legs at his voice, his

praise. I close my eyes and rest my head against him. We don't say anything until Neveah comes back and breaks up our cuddle by waving three five-dollar bills in her hand.

"This should cover it, I hope?" She looks at us and snorts. "You two keep doing you." She walks over to my purse and jams the cash inside, then puts her hands on her hips. "So, are we calling the campus police, or what?"

———

The process of working with the campus police is nothing like it was down at the local police department. I fill out forms and give a statement.

There are several very nice officers and an admin to whom I email the photos of the notes I've received since I left the originals back at the compound. They ask me about everything you could imagine—my routine, my schedule, my dating life. Any enemies I might have. They have me mark on a campus map which studio is mine, even though the studio was assigned by the college and they already have that information.

I try to be patient with every repeated question, every moment that I feel like I have to rehash the smallest of details again and again. I create a timeline of the last few weeks so many times, it all starts to blur.

They agree to communicate a confidential message to the Department of Residence Life indicating that they are aware that I may stay off campus while the matter is being investigated. When they ask where I intend to stay if I'm not in the dorms, I look to Josh.

I don't know what the right thing to say is. If I say my father's house, that puts him right in the middle of whatever is going on. I would rather face my stalker alone than put my father in harm's way. So, I sigh and give them the address of Josh's office. While it's not a residence, the campus police just need an address. The building has security cameras, and I notice Josh pull out his phone and send a few texts after I give that address.

I hope he's telling Alice to be watchful. I hate, literally hate, not knowing who I can trust. Worry that other people might be in danger because of me settles heavy in my chest.

By the time we finish with the campus police, I am exhausted. We never did eat lunch after those coffees, and now the sun is going down. We walk back to Josh's truck, his fingers lightly laced through mine. It's wild how right this feels. How normal.

But the sweet familiarity that we're building disappears the second we enter the parking structure. I tighten my hand around his as we approach the truck. I'm half worried his tires will be slashed or there will be some kind of letter tucked under the wipers. My heart rate picks up, and I look around worriedly. Josh has the same intense look on his face.

As I watch Josh scan the parking structure and then his truck, I realize we are in this together. And it feels more right than it should. It feels like something I want even when I'm not in danger. Although, who knows when I'll ever feel that way again. When it looks like things are clear and there are no obvious signs of trouble, he releases my hand.

"Hey." He unlocks the truck and holds open the passenger door for me. I stop between the warm wall of his body and the running board. "Annie?"

I look up at him, and my heart does a little flip in my chest. His eyes are so warm, so honest as he looks at me. It's as if I can see past the muscles and tattoos right into what's happening in his soul. He looks the same way I feel.

"Yeah?" I ask. I lift a hand to trace the bristles on his chin. I graze his thick lower lip with the tip of my thumb. "You're so hot," I whisper, a grin lifting half of my face. "I'm not trying to objectify you. I mean, I am. I can't imagine doing this with anyone else. I wouldn't want to. I'm also just really, really grateful that you were the only PI to take me seriously."

He closes his eyes for a second and parts his lips. "I do care," he says.

For a moment, we're just quiet.

I stroke his lip and then drop my hand. With a tired smile, I climb into the truck and fasten my seat belt. Josh closes the truck door and comes around to his side. He starts up the truck and rolls down the windows. I rest my elbow on the door, enjoying the air on my skin as the truck picks up speed.

The sun is setting, and the intense heat is softening, loosening its grip on the day. I tip my head toward my shoulder and close my eyes, letting the fresh air tease my hair. If we were really dating, what would we be doing tonight? Somehow, we feel so close despite the short time we've known each other. We skipped all the fuss of first dates, and we're already in the relationship zone.

I don't know where we're driving, and I don't ask. I trust Josh. I trust this feeling. I can be completely myself right now. Tired, confused, angry, scared. And hungry. A few minutes later, we pull into the parking lot of a mom-and-pop diner.

"You know me so well," I mumble, grinning. "Have you been here before? Or do you think the only places I eat are holes-in-the-wall?"

Ahead of us is a small strip mall. The lot looks pretty full, and there are loads of motorcycles parked right out front. Josh nods and points.

"Don't tell anybody, but this is Tiny's favorite place. Leo and his brother Tim brought me here a couple months ago, and we spotted Tiny eating alone. Good food." He comes around and opens the door for me. Totally not necessary, but I'm not going to complain or argue. I like that he's making an effort when it's obvious by the shadows under his eyes that he's tired too.

He didn't sign up for a round-the-clock job.

"I'll bet you miss your other clients right about now," I say softly, sliding past the running board.

Josh shuts the door and gives me a look. "Tailing cheating spouses and proving insurance fraud is nobody's idea of a good time." He curls a hand around my waist. "You are exactly my idea of a good time."

I give him a look and tuck my head against his shoulder. We head inside the diner, where there is a long line of people waiting for a table. Josh puts in our name, and then we head out to the parking lot to grab a bench and wait.

Before I can say anything, I notice Josh squinting, looking out over the parked cars.

"You okay?" I ask. "Anything wrong?"

He shakes his head then turns to me. "Tomorrow, we need to pay a visit to your dad."

I look down at my lap and clasp my hands together. "You think we need to? At this point, the police and the campus security office are involved. I mean…"

"Annie." Josh reaches into my lap and grabs my hands. "Whatever is going on is serious enough that he deserves to know. I'm going to keep you safe, but he should be aware. He could be…" Josh trails off, and the worry is back.

I groan. "We have to figure out why this is happening. Who's behind all this. There's no way I want to involve my father if there is a chance he could get hurt."

"Let's not take any risks." He nods, and then a text buzzes his phone, alerting us that our table is ready.

Inside the restaurant, I immediately see the enormous back of Tiny perched on a full-sized chair, sitting at a counter. I poke Josh and nod.

We head over to him, and Josh claps the big man on the back. "Good to see you," Josh says, then points to me. "We're grabbing a little dinner. See you later?"

Tiny lifts a chicken drumstick loaded with ranch dressing at us. "You breathe a word about this to Leo…" He sets the chicken down on his plate. "I'll work out some, but I'm not fucking giving up fried chicken for nobody."

Josh chuckles, then calls over a waitress who's standing behind the counter. He slips her a couple of twenty-dollar bills and points to Tiny. "His dinner's on us." Then he nods at Tiny before we follow the waiting hostess to our table.

The meal is great. It's no Pancake Circus, but I go for something a little lighter. Once I'm full, the fatigue hits, and I feel so tired, I could fall asleep. We're waiting for our check when Tiny heads out, signaling his goodbye with a single wave in our direction.

When the check comes, I move to grab my purse, but Josh stops me. "Let me get this, all right?" he says.

I nod, too tired to argue. I'll owe him so much when this is over. I may actually have to withdraw from school, not that I'll be able to get any of my tuition back.

Maybe Dad can spot me a small loan or give me my old job back. The thought of going back to work at the law office makes me sad. I thought I had one last chance to pursue my dream, but if I have to pay Josh back for all the time and expense... I could think of worse ways to have to do that.

Maybe I'm not ready for art school anyway. Maybe it's too late for someone like me to find her vision.

If all I ever am is a hobbyist, would that really be so bad? The purpose of art is to make people happy. And as much as I love my art, I just don't know if I want a life of galleries and hobnobbing. Of fancy parties and the pressure to produce work with a vision. Sometimes, yeah. The idea sounds like a dream. I would love to travel and have my work displayed all over the world. But the reality is that so few artists make even a modest living, let alone reach international success. And my very empty wallet reminds me that life doesn't accept payment in the form of dreams.

I watch Josh as he pays the bill. The waitress smiles at him and isn't exactly flirty, but she's definitely looking him over. She looks at me too, a friendly smile and an expression that makes me feel proud to be with him.

We head back to the truck, and I rest my head against the seat. I close my eyes and let all thoughts just drift away. I'm done thinking. All I want is to get home, take a hot shower, and climb into bed. Beside Josh. Who am I kidding... Just the idea that I'll be beside Josh again has me opening my eyes and sitting up straighter.

When I look his way, I see him narrowing his eyes and peering into the rearview. His arm muscles are tense, and his lips are thin.

"What is it?" I ask. "Anything wrong?"

I start to turn to look behind us, but his low voice stops me. "Look forward," he urges. "Don't look back. We're being followed."

The breath catches in my chest, and I grip the armrest between us. "Oh my God. Are you sure?"

He nods once. "A car followed us out of the lot at the diner. They're a couple car lengths back. I didn't get a good look at the driver."

"What should I do?" I ask. "Take a picture? Try to get the plate number?"

He nods. "Yeah. I'm going to find a place to pull

over where they'll have to pass us. You be ready. Got your phone?"

I grab it and unlock it, my hands starting to shake. I swipe to ready the camera and then try not to peek in the side mirrors.

"What kind of car?" I ask.

"White sedan," he says stiffly. "Two-door."

My hands start to sweat as Josh turns on his signal and eases over to the curb. He parallel parks quickly, then, with the truck still running, turns to face the street.

"I'm going to try too. On my word, hold up your camera." He grabs his phone and unlocks it. "Now."

I do as he says, peeking past him at the street. When a white car does go by, I try to snap a picture, but I just miss it. My heart's pounding in my chest.

"They sped up," I say. "I didn't get it. Are you sure, Josh? They were following us?" I look down at the picture I took, but it's just a blur. I ended up getting more of Josh's hand and his phone than the vehicle I was aiming at.

"It's all right." He nods. "I think I got it." He glares as he looks at the picture and zooms in on the image. The car has a small dent on the rear passenger panel. The driver looks like they are wearing a hoodie. "You recognize this?" he asks.

I shake my head. "I can't see anything. I can't make out the face or anything."

He sighs and leans back in his seat. He's staring down the street, the truck still idling, but the white sedan doesn't come back around.

"Annie," he says, turning to me. He looks more closely at the vehicle. "You may not recognize the driver, but do you recognize the vehicle? Is there any way this could be—"

"Who?" I blurt out, wiping my clammy hands on my legs. "Josh, who do you think this is?"

He firms his lips and looks down. "I'm pretty sure the driver was Neveah."

CHAPTER 14
ARROW

BY THE TIME we get back to the compound, Annie is a lot calmer. I haven't told her what I suspect yet. I can't bring this to her without more evidence. All I have right now is a hunch. I'm pretty damned sure that Neveah is not who she says she is. I've run into a few competitors in my line of work. People who go after bounties or work security. I have a nagging suspicion that Neveah is a PI and that she was the one following us.

But I'm not sure. The woman I vaguely remember is somebody I met years ago. She sure as shit didn't have pink buns in her hair back then either. But there is something about her face that's familiar. The way she seems sincerely protective of Annie and yet anxious to keep tabs on her at the same time. There's just no other way. Neveah has to be involved somehow. If not with the notes themselves, at least with whoever it is who has eyes on Annie.

I scan the dark yard around the compound, certain that no one has followed us here. Everything looks as

I'd expect, so we let ourselves in. We greet Midge, who's bustling around in the kitchen, cigarette pinched between her lips and cleaning gloves on her hands. Then we head into our room.

We sit on the end of the bed side by side, Annie's hands fisted in her lap.

"Hey," I tell her. "I'd like to ask you something, but it may make you a little uncomfortable."

Annie shifts on the bed and looks at me. "I don't think I could feel worse right now," she says, her voice shaky. "Someone was following us. What if they find us here? What then? What the fuck is happening?"

I turn to face her and take her hands in mine. "Listen to me, okay? I want you to really listen. I know this is scary, Annie. I know. The first time I was ever followed…" I lift my brows and chuckle softly under my breath. "Let's just say, once I was through the situation, I almost had to buy myself a new pair of jeans."

She gives me a half smile, and the sadness in her face makes my heart drop.

I meet her eyes. "I know how terrifying this is. You feel violated and vulnerable because some cocksucker has access to you, and you don't know what the fuck they want, where they will pop up next." I release her hands and smooth a few loose hairs back from her worried face. "You're looking over your shoulder constantly… It fucking sucks. I get that. But you're not defenseless, Annie. You've got me. I'm here for you. And I'm sure as shit not going to let anything happen to you. Not while there's breath in my body. Do you hear me?"

Her sky-blue eyes fill with tears, but she blinks them back and nods. "I'm scared, but more than that, I'm angry now," she whispers. "This is my life. I want it back. I want to think about my dad and have totally normal worries… Is he dealing with grumpy clients or a bad mood? I can't deal with all the secrets and danger. I want this to end, Josh. What do we do to make this stop?"

Whether she's ready or not, it's time to share my theory. I ask Annie to pull up Neveah's social media. She does, then shows me a well-curated feed of artsy shit.

I look at the follower count, the date of the first and most recent posts, and the noticeable lack of pictures of Neveah. Yeah, there are some recent ones of her wearing sunglasses, bright lipstick, hats, and shit to cover part or all of her face. But everything else on the profile could be fake.

"I don't think Neveah is who she says she is." As I admit this, I point to the feed on Annie's phone. "I doubt she would have had to spend even five hundred bucks to buy an aged account like this. It may have even come with the name Neveah."

Annie's face turns from worried to shocked. Her lips part, and she squints at me. "What do you mean? What the hell is an aged account?"

I explain how people can buy social media accounts. Accounts that give the impression you're a certain person. You can get almost anything for a price. You can make yourself look like an influencer with tens of thousands of followers. You can look like you've had a certain kind of lifestyle, backed up by a history of posts that support your claims. Aged accounts can be an easy way to create a past, an identity, or even sometimes, an alibi.

"But this one…" Annie swipes through each photo, closely inspecting the hashtags and comments. She clicks on the profile of one of Neveah's followers. "It looks like real people do follow her." She points to a post from three weeks ago. "I know this girl. She lives on my floor."

I nod. "Look before you started school. Go back six months. I'm sure plenty of profiles are real, but a lot will also be bots. The companies that create and sell these profiles aren't stupid. They know they have to make them look legit, and they do a damn good job of it."

Annie groans and tosses her phone on the bed. "So then, why…? Why would there be a private investigator posing as an RA in an art school? Is the school in on it? What about the art show that our adviser recommended for Neveah? Is nothing about my life real?"

I'd thought about that as well. It would be really tough to get into the position of RA on Annie's floor without major connections or money.

"Well, there's always a chance she got out of the investigations business and that she really is an aspiring artist now. Very few of us make it long-term, and I imagine a good-looking young woman like her might have had a hard time getting decent-paying clients. I know I have…"

The words slip out before I can stop them, and Annie shifts slightly away from me on the bed.

"Not you," I grit out. "Fuck, Annie. Listen. I'm sorry. Business has been down lately. That's why I was able to close my office and take your job for a steep discount. It may be a few weeks before I have another solid gig. It's not uncommon. And this is not about you. This is about why and how Neveah may be moonlighting as an RA."

She rubs her forehead like she's in pain. Her eyes are squeezed closed. She opens her eyes, and it's like a wave from the ocean bursts from the blue of her eyes and slams me in the heart. "You need work. You can't take me on as a charity case."

"You're not charity." I slide a hand beneath her hair and cup her neck. "Annie, it's not like that with us."

She draws her lower lip between her teeth as she sucks in a breath. "How is it with us, then?"

I lower my face to hers and crush her lips in a kiss. She laces her hands behind my neck and presses her chest against me. I taste her tongue against mine, our mouths open, no time for air or light or sound. All I feel is her beneath my hands. My eyes are closed, and I'm swimming—no, drowning—in her sweet flavor.

I release the kiss reluctantly, pulling my mouth away so I can breathe. I rest my forehead against hers. "No matter how this started, I'm in it," I tell her. "I'm in this with you. And I'm going to want you long after all of this is over. After I end it. Because I will, Annie. I'm going to end this so I can spend every morning and every night without you looking over your shoulder, wondering what's after you. The only one chasing you from now on is going to be me."

Her breathing is ragged, her cheeks flushed. "I'll never outrun the ass king," she murmurs. "Wouldn't even try."

I chuckle, but then we both grow serious again.

"So, what now?" she asks. "If Nevaeh isn't who she says she is, who the hell is she? And does she have anything to do with the notes?" Annie shakes her head. "I can't believe that she does. She seemed so genuinely surprised when I told her about them, Josh. I don't know what to think anymore."

"She may not know anything about the notes," I say. "But that doesn't mean she isn't working for the person who does. Someone hired her. Somebody who wants eyes on you. We just need to figure out who that is and what the hell they want."

Annie crinkles her brows. "Why would someone hire her to watch me but then not tell her about the notes?"

I sigh. "I can think of a lot of reasons. Plausible deniability, for one. She can't talk about what she doesn't know, Annie. And even if she's trained, experienced security, she's been posing as your friend. That's a hard thing to sustain long-term. She wasn't a cop, as far as I remember, and this is essentially an undercover operation."

"Who the hell has that kind of money?" she asks. "What could that cost? I mean, who is paying for that?"

I nod. I'd be lying if I didn't admit that I'd thought about that too. Big bucks. Which makes the question of what the person who hired Neveah thinks Annie owes them that much more confusing. The perp—the note-writer—hires someone to stay close to Annie so they can deliver extortion letters. Spending money to make money? That would mean whatever they've spent on Neveah... Fuck. They expect to get a lot more out of Annie.

I turn to her and hold her shoulders firmly. "Babe," I say. "Are you sure, one hundred percent sure, there's nothing I don't know about? No drug cartels in your past? No seven-figure embezzlement deals you and your dad were in on?"

I'm trying to make light of it, but I'm actually serious.

Annie's mouth drops open, and for a minute, she looks hurt.

She looks down at her flip-flops and curls her bare toes. "No, there's nothing," she finally says, shaking her head slowly. "Honest to God, Josh. I've racked my brain. I don't know. I just don't know. Do you not believe me?" She looks at me when say asks that.

"I believe every word you've told me." I stand and pull her toward me. "If you've missed something or forgotten something, it's not because you want to deceive me. I believe that. I believe you, Annie."

She lowers her forehead to my chest, and we stand together in Crow's bedroom. We're holed up in a motor-cycle club compound hiding out from a threat we can't fight because we can't find it. We're sitting ducks, and if there's one thing I refuse to do, it's stand by and let bad shit come to me. To someone I care about. To Annie.

"Tomorrow," I tell her. "We go to your father. We go back to that school. We confront Neveah and anyone and everyone we have to until we get answers. I'm done running. And I'm not going to let anyone chase you ever again."

————

Annie crawls under the covers in the same cupcake pajamas as the night before. I'm already there waiting. I'm doing some research on my phone, trying to find anything I can about Annie's adviser, June Crossard, and any scandals associated with the art school, but that's been a dead end. I was about to start digging into Annie's father when she came back from brushing her teeth.

"Want to watch something?" she asks softly, leaning her head against my shoulder.

"Your choice." I hand her the remote, and she flips through the channels, finally landing on a baking competition show.

"Do you bake?" I ask, settling back and expecting to watch some British people make jokes I don't understand while they make cakes I've never tried. I don't tell Annie, but I've watched every episode of every season of this show. Sometimes it's nice to take a break from life and crime, you know?

She points to the cupcakes on her shorts. "This is as close as I get to baking anything. Eating, on the other hand…"

She reaches out a hand and trails her fingers along

my forearm. I lift that arm, and she cuddles against my side. We watch the opening credits of the show and get through the bit at the beginning where the hosts rib one another, when Annie looks up at me intently.

"Babe," she whispers. "Are you into this show?"

I rumble out a laugh. "I've already seen every episode. I like to decompress to food TV."

Her eyes light up, and she pokes me in the ribs. "I had no idea. Do you bake?"

"Fuck no. That's part of the fun, though. This is shit I'd never, ever do. It doesn't stress me out because I have no skin in the game." I adopt a goofy, high-pitched British accent. "You'll never catch me bakin', luv."

She cackles loudly and then crawls out from under the light blanket. "I'm so glad," she says. "Because I really didn't want to watch anything anyway."

She tosses back the blankets, and the cool air hits my bare legs. I'm wearing boxer briefs again, and immediately, my cock starts to stiffen.

"What did you want to watch?"

She crawls over my legs and leans toward my ear. "I want to watch you fuck me."

At that, my dick goes from half-mast to fully awake. "I'm going to like that a hell of a lot more than watching bread proof."

She shoves my chest back lightly and gapes open her mouth. "You do watch this show."

We both laugh, and she strips off that cupcake top. Her hair falls loosely over her bronzed shoulders, and her tight nipples are so ripe, so hard, I want to suck them in my mouth like candies.

"Babe," I groan. "We didn't buy condoms."

She rocks back on her heels and then wiggles out of her shorts. She tosses the turquoise fabric to the floor, then jumps from the bed. She walks naked to her purse and slips a hand inside, then turns to me with a sultry grin. A little foil square is pinched between two fingers.

"I may have had a few in my dorm room…" she says, drawing her lower lip between her teeth.

"A few?" I echo, a shit-eating grin spreading across my face. I thank my lucky stars that in the mess of her dorm, she thought of snagging protection. "Let's not let that go to waste."

She crosses the floor naked, the light from the TV making her skin glow. I shove the covers aside, and she climbs in beside me and looks at up me. "This isn't too soon, is it?" Her words are soft. "I can put this thing right back where I…"

I silence the question by claiming her mouth with a kiss. A moan tears through her, rocketing blood to my cock. She sounds hungry, needy, and fuck, I'm feeling every whimper low in my gut. I taste her, kissing her until she's breathless and rubbing her thighs together.

"Lie on your back." I can hardly grit the words out. My dick is throbbing, and my lips are raw. I need to slow this down.

She scoots back on the bed, and I circle her wrists with my hands. She's still clutching the foil packet, so I leave it there. For now, she might just want to hold on to it. I'm not planning on needing it until she is wet and whimpering. I slide a leg between her knees, and she parts her lips. Her eyes are wide as she watches me settle carefully between her legs and lower my mouth to her tits. I'm still gripping her wrists as I trail the tip of my tongue against her tight peak. I plan on eating, licking, and sucking those tasty nipples until I have my fill.

I circle her nipple with my tongue, working my way around the tip.

She sucks air and squirms, then pants my name.

Fuck, she's soft, and even the taste of her skin under my lips is like heaven. Better than anything I've had and more mind-blowing than anything I could imagine. I don't care if I've known her six hours, six weeks, or six years…I want Annie Hancock.

I want her in a way that feels unsettling. Powerful and new and terrifying all at once. I don't think I'll ever want anyone else like this. I give in to the pull and nip her tight nipple between my teeth.

Her flesh ripples as the tiny hairs on her arms stand on end. Her heavy lids are lowered, her lips parted in a sensual pant. I kiss the fullness of her breast, the underside, between her cleavage, across her chest to the other tit, tightening my grip on her wrists.

"Too much?" I grunt, worried I might leave marks.

"No," she breathes. "More, baby. More."

I lower my mouth to the other breast and suck as much of it into my mouth as I can take. I work my tongue along her nipple, nibbling until a sheen of sweat breaks out along her hairline and she's panting hard.

"You like that?" I rasp against her skin. "I want you to come, Annie. I want you to come again and again for me."

She shudders a sigh. "More. Your beard."

I lower my chin to her delicate flesh and nod, letting the bristled stubble of my beard scrape her tender breast. I roll my neck so my roughness meets every inch of her most sensitive parts. Breast, scratch. Nipple, scrape. I tighten and loosen my hold on her wrists as I work her tits, until she wraps her legs around my waist and starts working her hips against me.

"Josh," she pants, her body flushed and hot. "I might…I might…"

I pivot my hips so my rock-hard cock is pressing against her center. I'm still wearing my briefs, and the friction seems to be just what she needs. I lower my chin to her breast and suck. Her hips thrashing against the mattress until she gives a tiny squeal and then trembles with release. Once she stills, I loosen my grip on her hands and rest my face against her breastbone.

"Keep going?" I ask. "I'm not planning on letting that go to waste."

She's loosened her grip on the condom packet, but it's still clutched in her palm.

"Hell no," she breathes. "I didn't dig this out of the ruins of my room for nothing."

I roll to my side and hold her close to me while she recovers from her orgasm. We watch the bakers drop cakes and encourage one another until, finally, Annie climbs onto her knees. She sets the condom packet beside me on the blankets and points to my briefs. "Sorry," she says. "I plan to block your view."

CHAPTER 15
ANNIE

"OFF, PLEASE." I point to Josh's boxer briefs. His chest is bare, the light from the TV highlighting the hairs that cover the contours of his muscles. He is gorgeous. His longish waves are messy, and I lean forward and smooth the hair back into place as I plant a kiss on his lips. "I can't wait to taste you," I tease.

Once his underwear is gone, I see his dick is already hard. "How do you want me?" he rasps.

I don't know what to say to that. I want him every way. His body, his heart. I look into his face, the dark eyes intently staring at me. His lips are curled in a smile, and fully naked, he's like my every wet dream come to life. Sexy, strong, protective.

For a moment, I remind myself that I hardly know this guy. But even as I think about it, I know it doesn't matter. I've had one-night stands. I've had boyfriends.

No one has ever made me feel the way he does. Protected. Wanted. Desired. Desirable.

I'm not worried about how I look or if my nails are

shaggy. I know he wants me, and the way I need him…
It's as real as anything I've ever felt. Whether it lasts a
day or forever, I have no hesitation.

I want Josh.

I want tonight.

I want this.

And if it's meant to last beyond the mess that is my
life right now, then I'll thank my lucky stars. I just can't
worry about the future when the only thing I trust right
now is what my mind, heart, and body are telling me.

And my body is telling me to stop wasting time
thinking about everything and start touching him.

I kneel between Josh's legs. He closes his eyes as I
slip my fingers around the base of his shaft. His cock
jerks, and I smile, lowering my face to blow soft kisses
against the head. He sucks in air and fists the blankets,
and I feel brazen, wild. I want him to watch me, to
touch me. To fist my hair and help me take him in.

"Josh." I whisper his name while I kiss his silken
shaft.

"Mmmm," he grunts.

"Save yourself for inside me."

He nods, the movement soft and relaxed. And then I
part my lips and drag the tip of my tongue along the
veined underside of his cock. He hisses and sighs, his
thick thigh muscles tensing. I watch him, my eyes open,
as I draw the head of his cock between my lips.

Licking the length of him gives me a feeling of utter
control. His thighs relax, his eyes close, and his hands
weave through my hair.

"Baby," he sighs. "Fuck. That's so good."

I roll my tongue from the base of him to the top, wetting his dick and stroking it in my closed palm. Once the tip is wet, I lower myself closer, settling onto my belly on the bed, and I use my hand to stroke his erection back and forth against my nipple. The tight skin is so sensitive, even the slight motion brings a rush of arousal between my legs. Josh responds too, panting and cursing lightly under his breath.

"I want to take you deep," I whisper.

I feel his fingers tighten in my hair, and I open wide then take as much of his length into my mouth as I can. I close my lips, swirl my tongue, and slowly pull my head back, tightening my lips against his shaft.

"Jesus, fuck," he grits.

I take that as an invitation to continue. He gently nudges my head, and I draw him deeper. Again and again, I pull his length into my mouth, licking and sucking until I feel a slight pulse from his cock.

"Babe," he warns, and I slowly pull my mouth away.

I fumble my fingers along the sheet until I feel the crinkle of the foil. I tear open the condom, toss the wrapper, and ease the thin latex over his length. He's panting and his eyes are open, liquid fire watching my every move. I kneel again, crawling up his legs until my pussy is centered over him. I bend down so my face is level with his, and I meet his eyes.

"Hey," he whispers.

"Hey back."

Something passes between us then. Something soft and sweet. A touch of shyness, maybe on my part.

I lean forward and stroke his face. The beard that just a few minutes ago brought me to the edge and over. "Josh." I whisper his name and lean forward. I touch my lips to his, not sure what to expect.

He kisses me back. But it's not needy, voracious. His lips are soft, and his words thick with emotion.

"Annie," he whispers, my name sounding so damn beautiful in the throaty rasp. "You're fucking unbelievable. You're perfect."

I smile, shaking my head at the compliment. I'm far from perfect, but I know what he means. I think I feel the same thing he's feeling. This. Us. That's what's unbelievable. The kind of perfect I've never felt before but have craved with my whole soul.

Whether this lasts forever or just until I'm out of danger, I'm in it. I'm his. And I believe he's mine too.

I grin, ready to give to him exactly what he gave me. I settle over his cock, then lower myself until I feel the head nudge my wet opening.

The sensation sends sparks from my belly to my toes. The loving moment has passed, and I'm fully aroused again. Wanting my body to express things my heart isn't ready to.

I clench my pussy around the tip of his erection and then lift myself up and off him. I don't settle deeper, but pull away, then I relax my muscles, slide down onto him, and tighten, milking just the head of his cock with my pussy. Over and over, I slide just over the head and then back up, up and down until he's thrashing beneath me.

"Fuck," he bites out. His aroused curses send a flood of wetness to my core.

I run a hand along his chin and touch his parted lips. I want to take my time, savor every moment of our first time. The first time we'll join our bodies and share something that will bind us. Maybe even bind us for the long run. I want to enjoy every second, but more than anything, after everything that's happened the last few days—the fear, the running, the uncertainty—I want to make this pleasure last. But I don't think Josh can hold out for much longer.

He leans forward, plants his hands on my hips, and tilts his hips up. I relax my legs and slide down until we are fully joined. His length is all the way inside me, our bodies connected in pleasure that is so far beyond exquisite, it's almost painful. As I adjust to his length, I lean back just slightly, pivoting my weight until I feel pressure in the right spot.

"Baby, ride me hard," he begs.

The space between us closes as he lowers his mouth to my breast. He pulls a nipple into his mouth and sucks hard while I rock my hips against his.

He's so deep inside me, every roll of my hips has his shaft sliding against my walls. The power of his mouth on my nipples would be enough to send me off into oblivion. The angle of his shaft while I ride puts pressure on my clit. I go boneless in seconds.

I close my eyes and ride his body, rocking and gentle until I find my pace, and then I go frantic, digging my toes into the mattress and clawing at his back as I chase our perfect high.

"Oh God. Oh my God." I'm about to fall over the edge. I see the cliff coming, and I careen toward it, eyes closed, Josh's teeth tearing at my nipple while my legs widen, and I toss my head back.

When the climax hits, it's like a thousand spotlights are turned on behind my eyelids. I squint against the colors, crying out with the crest of every wave. I ride him until my thighs burn and my heart rate slows. I whimper his name as my head rolls forward, coming to rest against his shoulder.

"So fucking good," he mumbles. "Good girl. Now give me that ass."

I need his help to lift off his cock and lie on my belly. I feel like my bones are made of jelly, and it's the best feeling ever. My pussy is hot and swollen, my nipples so raw, the pressure of the rough sheets bringing another wave of sensation over my body. I flop my arms across the bed like a rag doll while Josh slips a pillow under my abdomen.

Then I feel the smack of his palm against my ass.

"Fuck," he breathes. "Your body… You're goddamn perfect, Annie."

Then I feel his palm come down on my cheek again. Even as wrecked as I am, the sensation feels amazing. I lie there and take it, accepting it, receiving every sensation he wants to give me. He curls his fingers around my ass, and I don't even have the strength to resist or tense up when I feel him spread my cheeks.

I wonder vaguely what he wants to do, if he's going to do something there or just look, but I don't have time to feel insecure. I feel the lightest touch of his fingertip circling my ass. I have never, ever been touched there, but I've always been curious about what it would feel like.

I don't have time for emotions or reactions because all I feel is the lightest pressure, almost a tickle as he touches my asshole and spreads my cheeks farther.

"Someday soon, baby," he tells me. "I'm going to make every inch of your body mine."

I groan into the sheets, something that might be a word if I had the strength to shape the sound into actual syllables. It's yes, please, and more, all wound into a grunty thing that makes Josh laugh. My ass is propped up slightly by the pillow, and I don't even feel shy that he's seeing my most private everything.

All I want is this.

I trust him.

I want him.

I am completely falling for him.

By the time I feel the head of his cock nudge my pussy, I'm wet again, or still… I don't know and I don't care.

He teases my lips a little like I teased him, entering me, then pulling out. Going deeper, pulling back. I thought I was too wrung out to even use my legs, but turns out I'm wrong. With Josh behind me, agonizing me with teasing little thrusts, I shove my hips back toward him, desperate to have him fill me again.

He obliges, thrusting slow, but this time pushing until he can't go deeper. I feel him fill me so completely, I open my mouth and practically bite the sheets, humming his name and pressing my hips back to take him deeper than it seems possible to do.

He leans forward and grips my shoulders, then rockets his hips back and forth, using my shoulders for leverage.

My body is bouncing in time with his, the resistance his weight creates completely overpowering me. I give in to every sensation and just feel him. The rock-hard muscles of his legs between mine. His strong hands. His cock. Our bodies move together in a powerful effort that sends me to the brink of another orgasm, but I won't reach a third. I can't.

I'm lost to so many feelings. Lost to this magnetic connection we have. His body riding mine, mine rocking with his.

"Annie, fuck," he cries, thrusting so hard, I swear we're moving the bed.

When he's done, sweaty and breathless, he rolls to the side, shoves aside the pillow that was under my belly, and flops onto his back. He peels the condom from his softening erection and rolls it tightly into a ball and sets it on the floor. I imitate his flop, struggling to find the energy to roll to my back, but wanting to get closer to him.

He opens his arms, and somehow my limbs cooperate. I slam my cheek against his chest and huff a sigh.

"I brought more condoms." I can barely form the words to remind him, but I mumble it against the heat of him, my eyes closed, my body happy.

Then I pass out, every inch of me falling into an exhausted, blissful sleep.

CHAPTER 16
ARROW

I WAKE up and my body is plastered against Annie's, and if I'm not sweating from where our legs intertwine, my arm is asleep from trying to hold her close. I don't give a shit if it's the worst night's sleep of my life. I've never ever felt this fucking good. Every time I squint my eyes open against the dark, I'm reassured she's here.

I've dated plenty and slept with plenty more. But I've never had a connection with a woman on a personal and physical level so fast. So powerful. Not only do I fucking love her company, her humor, her sweetness, but goddamn, she is wild in bed.

I resist the urge to wake her in the middle of the night for another round of fun, but by the time the sun brightens the windows, I feel her fingers stroking my morning wood.

"Hey," she whispers, looking up at me. Her hair is tousled, and she has the cutest little sleep lines pressed into her right cheek. I stroke the skin with a finger.

"Hey to you, gorgeous. Sleep okay?"

She ducks her chin to kiss my fingers and shakes her head. "It was the worst night of sleep I've had in a while, but it was still the best night ever."

I chuckle. "Same, babe. Same."

We lie together in a groggy fog, her fingers exploring my chest and abs while I smooth her hair and try to control the raging erection that presses against her thigh. She cuddles closer, her thigh thrown over mine, and my dick throbs in response.

She cups my balls and gently strokes my sac. "My purse is right over there…"

That's all the invitation I need. "I'm going to bring every single condom you packed," I tell her.

I ease out of bed, my boner bobbing painfully as I head to her open purse. I reach inside her small purse and feel the loose cash that Neveah stashed in there yesterday. I fumble around past a wallet and ChapStick, but before I feel the familiar foil-wrapped packet, my fingers hit on something small, flat, and hard. I pick up her purse and open it wide, peering inside.

"Did you find them?" Annie calls. She's naked on the bed now, the sheets pushed aside as she watches me with a sly grin on her face.

"Can I look in here?"

She cocks her head and looks at me with a concerned expression. "Yeah, why? What is it?"

I fish my way to the bottom of her purse and stop when my fingers hit the small disk again. As soon as I pick it up, my gut turns over, and I break into a sweat.

I hold up the small device to show her. "Is this yours?" I ask.

Annie's eyes widen. "What is that?" she asks. "I don't even know what it is. And no, it's not mine."

She climbs out of bed naked and meets me at her purse. She peeks inside where the loose cash is on top. I can see now that I look that two condoms, their perforated ends still connected, have folded together and are wedged between the flaps of her wallet. I pull those out and set them on the dresser.

"We'll hang on to these," I tell her. "But I think we'd better get dressed."

She holds out a hand for the device I found in her purse. "Josh, what the hell is that?"

I knit my brows together and rub my eyes with two fingers. "This, Annie, is a tracking device."

She staggers away from me, clutching her hands to her bare chest. "Shut up," she says, shaking her head. "No. No, it can't be. How did it get there?" She stares at me, her golden hair still messy from sleep and sex.

She's looking to me for answers, but I have nothing but questions. I hold the device in my hands. "I'm going to talk to Tiny," I say, striding over to the bed and pulling on my briefs. "Until we know what's going on, the compound may not be safe."

Annie sinks down on the bed and covers herself with the end of the sheet. "No…" she whispers, shaking her head. "I can't believe it."

I place the device back in her purse, then turn to kneel in front of her. "Annie." I grip her knees in my hands and squeeze. "These guys are going to be okay. They aren't just old dudes who go for joyrides together. Until not that long ago, the Disciples spent more than their fair share of time on the wrong side of the law. Tiny and the rest of them can hold their own."

Her eyes are bright with tears. "Neveah?" She croaks out the word, and the raw sadness in her eyes cracks my heart into a million pieces.

I nod. "Shower and get dressed. We're going back to campus."

———

By the time we're both dressed and grabbing a cup of coffee from the kitchen, the entire compound is on high alert.

Tiny stands shoulder to shoulder with Dog and Eagle in the kitchen.

"Crow was on a job, but he's on his way," he tells me with a nod. "Morris is at the office with Alice. I told Leo to let his brother handle the shop. He's sticking close to my daughter just in case. We've got the compound covered. Nobody will come in or out without us knowing about it." Tiny laces his thick fingers together and cracks his knuckles. "I'm looking forward to protecting what's mine. Whatever it takes."

Annie opens her mouth to say something but stops. She looks from Tiny to Dog to me, and then down at her shoes. "I can't believe this." Her voice is almost a whisper.

Tiny grimaces, and the sight's definitely scary. He plants a meaty fist on the counter and nods at Annie. "You listen to this one," he says, gesturing to me with his other hand. "That's your only job. Listen to Arrow and stay safe. Don't you worry about anything else."

He nods at me, and I return the gesture. I don't know how I'm going to thank them for offering us shelter. Being willing to risk whatever danger this is to give us a place to stay. I shove that thought to the back of my mind and focus on what we need to do.

The first priority is confronting Neveah.

Annie's hands shake as she sips her to-go mug of coffee, and I wrap a hand around her waist.

"Besides," Tiny says. "The sooner you two can get back to your own place, the sooner we can sleep in peace."

Annie's eyes widen in horror as Dog taps his fingers on the kitchen paneling. "Thin walls," he laughs.

While Annie practically blushes herself into next week, I shake my head.

"We'll keep in touch," I tell them. "Do the same. Anything we need to know about goes down, you know how to reach me."

Before I take Annie outside to the truck, I scan the perimeter for cars, people, for anything that might be lying in wait for us. She stands back behind the closed door while I inspect my tires and start the truck. It all seems safe, but I have to assume that whoever placed that tracker and whoever she's working for know exactly where we are.

Before I wave Annie over, I drive up and down the long driveway, testing my brakes and listening to my truck for any unfamiliar sounds. Everything seems to be working fine. Nothing seems to be tampered with, and the brake lines obviously haven't been cut, so I drive back and idle as close to the door as I can.

"Come on," I call, rolling down the passenger window.

Annie takes off running from the front door of the compound, fear etched on her beautiful features. She climbs onto the running board and slams the door shut behind her, then quickly rolls up the window.

"I'm so sorry," she says again. "This is…" Her voice trails off as she gazes out the window.

I reach a hand across the divider and squeeze hers. "Annie, stop apologizing. This isn't your fault. We're going to get answers from Neveah. And we're going to get them today."

We make the rest of the drive back to campus in silence. My gut is churning as I think through how long that tracker was in Annie's purse. She'd been using a backpack until yesterday, so I'm sure the device was just placed there when I left Neveah to get coffee. I'm not sure if I regret that decision or if that was the smartest thing I've done. If Neveah denies leaving the device, it's not like I can rough her up to get her to confess, but I'll figure that out when we get to her.

We park in student parking and use Annie's student tag, then hurry into the dorms. I peek at the security cams over the doors as we enter, wondering just how deep this danger runs. I glare at the cameras and lace my fingers through Annie's. Every student we pass gets a sour look as I search every face, every hand, every passing shape for clues. Most of the students seem too relaxed to even notice us.

It's a gorgeous day. Sunlight floods the dorm lobby as everyone has someplace to be. I want that for Annie. I want carefree, artistic, sunshine Annie, and I'm going to get that back for her.

We head upstairs and go right to Neveah's.

"Let me talk to her," I say, lifting my hand to pound on her door.

I knock three times, loud and hard.

Annie stands beside me, her hands clasped together and a look of absolute fear on her face.

"You going to be okay?" I ask. "Do you want to go to your room and wait? I'll handle this, Annie."

She shakes her head and instead pushes past me. "I'm mad. I want to know what's going on." She pounds on the door, calling Neveah's name. "It's Annie. Open up!"

A door across the hall from Neveah's opens, and a young woman peeks out at us. "Annie? What's the matter?" She looks me over and cocks her chin at me. "You looking for Neveah?"

Annie turns and talks to the girl. "Yeah," she says, without bothering to introduce me or explain. "It's kind of urgent. Have you seen her?"

The girl shakes her head. "I actually haven't seen her since last night. We were going to grab dinner together, but she bailed. I texted her around seven to see if she was okay, and she just said yeah, she got held up thrift shopping and would talk to me later." The girl shrugs. "I haven't seen her today, though."

The girl tells Annie that if she sees Neveah or hears

from her, she'll let Annie know. Annie turns to me. "I'm going to text her. Tell her it's urgent."

I nod, and we head toward Annie's room. I'll admit, my mind first thinks about how many more condoms she's got stashed in there. But any R-rated thoughts leave my brain as soon as we walk through the door. Right underneath our feet is a note.

"Annie," I say, nodding. "Don't touch it."

We enter the room and close the door slowly behind us, then we bend over the letter to inspect it.

"Something's off," Annie says, squinting. "It's not like the others."

I've already seen that. This note is printed on plain white paper. Annie's entire name—first and last—is printed in blocky black ink on the outside. There is no envelope, and the regular sheet of white paper is folded in half.

"Should I read it?" she whispers. "Or call campus security?"

I know there are no security cameras inside these hallways, so unless the exterior building cams picked up someone carrying this note very visibly and obviously, I'm not sure there is anything they can do to help us figure out who left this.

"We're going to read it," I tell her. I bend down and pick up the note, then look to Annie. "Okay?"

She nods and swallows hard. "I'll do it."

I hand the note to her, and she opens it.

Annie, you and your tattooed fuck buddy are not smart enough to get you out of this. When you get this note, text me at the number below. I'll give you instructions from there.

She holds up the note, and I grab my phone, immediately doing a lookup on the number that's at the bottom. "That's not Neveah's number, is it?" I ask.

She shakes her head. "Let me check. I think Neveah has a local area code. This is one I don't recognize."

"Probably a burner." I'm not able to find anything online in a quick search of the number, except to confirm that the area code is not local.

"Should I call Neveah? Text her?" she asks. She's holding the note like it's poisonous.

"No," I tell her. "If this is a burner phone, I'm going to guess they don't have your number in their contacts. Leave the tracker from your purse here in your room. Then we'll text this number when we're far from campus. If whoever left this note is tracking us, I don't want them to have any idea where we are when we text."

Annie wrinkles her nose. "Should we take it with us and, like, throw it out of the truck? What if whoever is behind all this comes to campus, thinking I'm here?"

I agree she has a good point. "I have an idea," I tell her. "Come on. Keep the tracker. I want Neveah to know we're on the move."

We take the note and, with the tracker in Annie's purse, we head back to my car. I grip her hand tightly in mine and keep an eye on our surroundings. I don't want to involve campus security at this point, but I do know who I need. I don't have many close friends, but I do have a few I can count on. And I'm going to need backup.

————

An hour later, we pull into the parking lot of the strip mall that houses my office.

"Come on." I climb out of the driver's seat and come around to open Annie's door. We inspect her car for any evidence that it's been touched or tampered with, but I don't see anything.

Annie follows me to the doggie day care first. Leo is holding baby Rider and watching as Lia chats on the phone with a customer.

"Hey, Arrow," Leo greets me and then waves at Annie. "How's it going, man?"

I give a small smile to the squirming toddler, who seems to be teething hard since he's chewing like mad on a tiny plastic toy that's shaped like a banana. "Can we talk when you and Lia have a second?"

Leo nods and waves to Lia, who's got a phone clutched between her shoulder and ear while she talks. Lia finishes up her conversation and hustles to greet us.

"Hey." She's breathless and happy, her apron tied tight around her waist. She gives me a quick hug and then leans in to hug Annie. "I don't know you, sweetie, but I hear you're staying at my dad's?"

Annie looks at me, and I make the introductions. "Annie, this is Lia, Tiny's daughter." Once the intros are out of the way, I fill Leo and Lia in on the shortest possible version of the story. "We have no idea why

Annie is being tracked, but I want you all to be aware."

Lia's brows knit together. "I'll close the shop to appointments only," she says. "I won't let anyone in or out unless I know them or they have a dog already here to pick up."

I nod. "That's a good plan."

"Tim's in the shop," Leo says, "but he can handle himself. I'll tell him so you don't have to waste time. Talk to Morris yet?"

I shake my head. "That's my next stop."

We say our goodbyes and head toward my office. It's only been a few days since I locked up, but it feels like forever. As we pass by Alice's office, I can see Morris leaning over his wife's shoulder, reading something up on her computer screen.

"Come on." I take Annie's hand, and we push open the office door.

Morris lifts his head and shoves his glasses up onto his forehead. "Arrow," he says with a nod. "Annie, how you doin', sweetheart?"

Alice jumps up from her desk and pulls Annie into a hug. "Sweetie, what's going on? Tiny called this morning and said the trouble may not be over."

I explain everything. I wouldn't normally bring anyone into the specifics of a case like this, but Morris stuck his neck out by letting us stay at the compound. And now the very danger that sent me into hiding there may have found us. And worse, may know where we are at all times. There's no more hiding. He deserves to know what I do so he can protect his own.

Morris is quiet as I explain what we do know, as well as what we don't. He puts the stem of his glasses between his teeth and thinks for a minute. Then he looks from Annie to Alice and back to me.

"What're you thinking? What's your plan?"

I explain the note and the fact that we need to text this burner phone for instructions. Morris nods and then tells Alice to lock up the office.

"What are you doing?" I ask, confused why they're locking up.

"A threat to any of us is a threat to all of us," he says. "We're coming with you."

CHAPTER 17
ANNIE

I DON'T KNOW where we're going or what we're doing, but once we're back inside the office where I first met Josh, I throw myself into his arms. "I don't want anyone to get hurt," I murmur against his chest.

He's wearing a black shirt and dark jeans. The fabric of his shirt is so soft, and I wish I could close my eyes and stay here, breathing in his spicy cologne and fresh soap smell. But I can't. I can't pretend whatever this is hasn't changed. Things are going to get worse before they get better. I just have to believe they will get better. And that in the end, we're all going to be okay.

Josh leans back and lifts my chin so our eyes meet. "Nobody is going to get hurt," he vows. "Tiny's at the compound, and Leo will look out for Lia and Rider. You have me, and I'm not going to let anything happen to you. You know that, don't you?"

I nod. I do know. I mean, of course I believe that. It's just that this has gotten so big. So out of hand. So many more people are involved, and I still don't have any answers.

"Knock knock." Morris peeks his head into the office. Alice trails just a few paces behind. "All right, Arrow. What's the plan?"

Josh releases me, and I grab my phone.

"I'm going to have Annie text the number from the last note. We'll make a plan when they reply." He looks at me and nods. "You ready, babe?"

I open my phone and punch in the number from the note. Then I type out the message Josh and I talked about on the drive over.

Who are you, and what do you want from me?

Then, I immediately text Neveah. Josh thought it would be useful to see which number responded first, and to see what, if anything, Neveah said.

Neveah, I'm in trouble. Are you around?

I hit send, putting two messages out into the world that might just change everything. If I'm lucky, they will both respond. I'm not even sure what I hope for. Part of me hopes Neveah answers fast and answers first. I so desperately want to believe she has no part in whatever all this is. But as the seconds pass by, I have to start accepting that she is probably not the person I think she is. She might be someone who's never cared about me. Who's meant harm to me all along.

I don't have the heart to feel sad. I don't have tears for the friendship I lost. I'm scared. Angry. And more than anything, I am motivated. I want answers. I want to end this.

The number I don't recognize texts back first.

Lobby of the Royal Garden Hotel. Two hours. Tell your tattooed, jerk-off boyfriend he's not going to be a hero today.

Hands shaking, I hold out my phone to Josh.

"I don't think this is Neveah…"

Josh takes my phone and reads the message. "Nothing from her?" he asks. "Just this?"

I nod.

Josh starts pacing the floor. He runs a hand through the front of his hair and tugs on it in frustration. "All right, here's what we know. Someone wants something from you. Let's assume they hired Neveah to keep tabs on you until they get what they want. They know about me, and they still want access to you. We have to assume at this meeting, they'll be armed. Dangerous."

"But what do they expect?" I ask. "That I'll hand over my debit card and PIN? I don't have anything. I don't know anything."

"We have to assume there is more than one person involved," Josh says. "Neveah might still be involved. She probably carries a firearm."

"A gun?" I squeal the word. Suddenly, the room starts to spin. I drop into one of Josh's office chairs and cover my face with my hands. "A gun," I mutter. "A fucking gun."

"Annie." Josh's voice is calm as he puts his hands on my shoulders. He stands behind me and squeezes gently. "We're going to be in the lobby of a crowded, upscale hotel for a reason. They're not going to try to open fire in a place like that. There are cameras, security." Josh shakes his head. "To be honest, it doesn't make any sense. It's like they want to lure us away from something."

Morris interrupts then. "Could be they plan an ambush. You may never make it inside the lobby. If they know what you drive, there could be people along the route lying in wait."

Josh nods. "Yeah, or they could plan on taking us at gunpoint from the scene to a bank, to hold us for ransom. Anything is possible."

"Ransom…" The word echoes in my ears, and I blurt out a violent laugh. "I can't believe any of this. Who the hell is this, and what do they want?"

"Only one way to find out." Morris paces the office, looking from me to Alice. "Bait and switch."

Josh looks confused, but it's Alice who asks what he means.

Morris nods at his wife. "You put on a pair of sunglasses, at a distance, you're a dead ringer for Annie." He chuckles and scrubs a hand through his hair. "I'm no pretty boy, and these grays won't fool anybody who knows Arrow. But what we can do is send Alice in place of Annie. Arrow stays close to Alice to convince this fuckwad she's Annie. Meanwhile, I'm in the shadows with eyes on my old lady."

Alice looks at me. "It's a good plan. Josh will be with me the entire time, and Morris will be close by. Whoever wants to get close to you might reveal themselves. By the time they realize I'm not you, Morris will have the guy on his knees."

"If I don't get to them first." Josh's arms are crossed,

and his jaw is set. "If it's Neveah, Annie, are you going to be able to call the cops on your friend?"

I look down at my phone. There's still no response from Neveah.

"Yeah," I say quietly. "I won't hesitate." If she is the one behind this—or if she's involved at all, of course. I want this nightmare to end.

Josh starts rummaging through his desk drawers. "I'm going to want Annie to have eyes on Alice the entire time," he says. "If there is someone you recognize in that lobby—anyone, I don't care who it is—you say the word."

I can't believe this is happening.

Morris pulls his cell phone out of his pocket. "I'm going to make some calls. If I'm going to send my wife into the line of fire, I want more than your scrawny ass on my back."

Josh nods, but he's busy unlocking a drawer and pulling out equipment like we're in some kind of spy movie. I can't believe this is happening. A week ago, my biggest worry was that I had no idea what kind of artist I wanted to be. Now, I'm in the middle of some kind of shakedown?

I walk around Josh's desk and grab his arm. "Josh, wait." I shake my head, a sick feeling rising in the back of my throat. "Maybe we should go to the police. Bring them this latest note and show them the text from the burner phone. It can't possibly be safe to do this alone."

He turns to face me, looking flustered for just a second. Then he puts down everything he's gathered from his desk and pulls me into his arms. "Annie," he says. "If we go to the police, they won't be able to mobilize any kind of presence in two hours. Not with this note. There is no demand, no threat of bodily harm. The person doing this knows what they are doing. They didn't demand money. I've been chasing down bad guys for a while. There is nothing in this text or that note that would justify a police response." He meets my eyes, and I know from the intensity there that he's worried. Concerned. Maybe even scared. "This is on me. I'm the person you've entrusted to help you. And I'm going to make sure nothing happens to you or Alice or anyone else. But you've got to work with me, and you've got to trust me. Do you, Annie? Do you trust me?"

I look up at the man I didn't know existed a week ago. Six months ago, I didn't know Neveah. So much has changed so fast in my life. But I believe in my heart that of all the crazy shit that's happened, the one thing I can put my faith in is Josh.

"I trust you," I whisper. I close my eyes and squeeze him one long, last time. Then I release him and lift my chin. "Tell me the plan."

———

The Royal Garden Hotel is absolutely beautiful. An upscale boutique hotel, it has a white stucco exterior with thick red Spanish tiles on the roof. It's a small hotel with a U-shaped drive and a glistening fountain up front. Valets in matching golf shirts greet guests as they pull into the drive and park their cars, unload luggage, or offer assistance to visitors to the small tearoom that's open to the public. Morris and I park on the street two blocks away and walk toward the valets.

I've changed into a dress that I bought from a discount store near the strip mall and a pair of sandals. I've got a large sun hat on to cover my hair which is styled in a bun underneath. The brim of the hat is wide and covers the wireless earpiece I'm using to communicate with Josh.

"We're here," I say. There is no clicking sound or anything. Just Josh's gentle voice in my ear.

"Look for me. Northwest corner of the lobby, table closest to the door, babe," he says. "Alice and I are both seated. She's facing me, and I'm facing the exit."

I'm wearing sunglasses and holding Morris's arm like he's my date. In the crook of my elbow, I'm carrying the purse with the tracking device we found. We figured if the device was not in the same place I was, whoever was keeping tabs on me might figure out this was a setup. As we walk up to the valets, I literally feel like every eye is on me. I feel exposed, even though I'm in the shadow of a hulking tattooed man whose wife is filling in for me.

It's terrifying and strange, and I have never, ever felt this kind of danger. I immediately wish Josh would get out of this business. How many times has he done something like this? Putting himself in actual physical danger? The fact that someone in this hotel could be armed and ready to hurt me… I feel slightly dizzy with panic.

Morris turns to me and steadies me with a hand.

"You've got this, darlin'. I'm right here." His eyes crinkle at me when he smiles, and a little bit of my heart melts. I've never had friends like this. Friends who would put themselves and those they love in harm's way. These bikers are a lot more like the guys on TV than they initially let on. Caring, sexy, fearless. I try to gather my strength as Morris leads me toward the valets.

"Afternoon," he says politely. "We were hoping the tearoom has space for two."

One of the valets grins and holds open the door. "Of course, sir. You can check with the hostess. The tearoom is straight through the lobby."

We walk through the doors, and the first person I see is Tiny. He's wearing a plain short-sleeved black shirt, and he's never looked as big as he does in the elegant, sun-drenched lobby. I'm glad I'm wearing sunglasses so he can't see my eyes follow him. Tiny doesn't look up even as Morris and I pass. He's reading a newspaper, and for a second my stomach sinks.

Who are we fooling, playing this spy game? Tiny reading a paper sticks out like a sore thumb. If anyone had been keeping an eye on the compound, they would recognize him.

"Let's just keep walking, sweetheart." Morris's voice is low and calm. He claps a hand over my hand that is now digging my nails into the crook of his elbow. "You're doing great."

I nod and look straight ahead, scanning the place through the dark sunglasses for anyone I recognize. I see Dog and Eagle, the two bikers from the compound, but I almost don't recognize them. They are wearing neon-yellow construction T-shirts and hard hats. To anyone not paying attention, they look like they belong here. They're standing together, pointing out the large plate glass windows, looking like they are deep in conversation.

Morris ushers me down the steps that lead into the lobby, where a few small tables and chairs are filled with guests. Some are sipping to-go cups of coffee with luggage seated on the floor beside them. A mother stands over a little boy who is swinging his legs and playing on a tablet.

Children. There's a child here.

"Morris," I whisper, knowing that Josh can hear everything I say through the earpiece. "There's a little boy and his mom…"

"Uh-huh. I see 'em." He steers me deeper into the lobby, and we walk carefully down a set of tiled steps.

I scan the lobby and see the front desk staff, a concierge, but no sign of any type of security. No police. God, I pray that Josh is right.

Morris slows his steps and pulls a phone out of his pocket. "Excuse me a minute, darlin'."

I don't know if his manners are part of the act, but while Morris picks up the call, just fifty feet ahead of me, I see the familiar form of my PI. He's wearing an unusual set of sunglasses, ones that I know have the ability to record what he's seeing. The battery on the glasses only lasts an hour—I know because Josh told me he wasn't going to put them on until shortly before my stalker is set to arrive.

Morris ends his call and then speaks loudly enough for anyone listening nearby to hear. "The tearoom said they'll have a table for us in about fifteen minutes. Do you want to wait, or should we go someplace else?"

I panic for a minute, not being entirely sure what he wants me to say. I look at Morris, and his face is calm, his smile sincere. "I'd really like to wait, sweetheart. Maybe we can hang out here in the lobby?"

"Oh yeah. Yes, yes. Let's wait," I say.

My heart is racing, and my stomach is clenched tight with fear. I try not to look at every person in the hotel, but all of a sudden, the place seems so loud, so full.

I'm overwhelmed by what to do, how to act. But there's no time to second-guess the plan. The two hours have passed, and I have four bikers, a biker's old lady, and a PI at my side. I'm not alone. Whatever is about to happen, I'll handle it. All I can do is pray that we all come through this okay.

I didn't ask Josh if Morris or any of the bikers are armed. I know Josh isn't carrying a weapon, but he assured me he would take down anybody who tried to hurt me—or Alice playing me—with his bare hands. My hand starts to sweat, and the hat on my head feels too big and itchy. My skin is crawling, and I notice Josh lean forward across the table and whisper in Alice's ear.

Alice could truly pass for my twin. She's even wearing the clothes I took off after grabbing this maxi at the Dress For Less near the strip mall. Her hair looks a little blonder than mine is, but even to someone who knows me well, it could just be the sunlight. With sunglasses of her own, my tank and shorts, and her hair in a loose ponytail, even I could believe she is me.

I feel Morris's body tense when Josh leans close to her, and I have to hold back a smile. These bikers really do protect their own. I can almost hear the ear-blasting I expect Morris to give Josh for carrying the ruse out just a little too convincingly.

"Anything?" Josh's voice comes through my earpiece, and I pretend like I'm talking to Morris.

"Nope, but I'm looking around." I pretend to pick lint off Morris's shirt so I can look over his shoulder at the crowd around him.

Suddenly, I do see someone who looks vaguely familiar. "That's weird," I murmur, staring just past Morris. The man in the business suit is walking right toward Alice.

"You see something?" I hear Josh's voice in my ear and feel Morris tense beside me.

"Yeah, but this can't be who we're waiting for. That looks like my father's law partner." I'm squinting through my sunglasses. I want to move the dark shades from my face, but if I do, anyone looking for me will see my whole face.

Before I can look back to confirm what I'm seeing, my phone buzzes in my purse.

"Fuck," I breathe.

"Darlin, I think you should answer that," Morris says.

"Annie?" I hear a familiar voice address not me, but Alice.

"Talk to me, not her." Josh stands and addresses the

man. My hand shakes violently as I reach into my purse. The man approaching Josh is my father's law partner, Martin Engler. And the person whose contact is coming up on the caller ID?

It's Neveah.

CHAPTER 18
ARROW

"DON'T TALK TO HER," I say, rising to my feet, my voice mean. I look through the shaded safety glass, making sure the tiny camera embedded in the frames focuses right on this man. "You talk to me."

Alice lowers her chin and ducks her head, refusing to look at the man and keeping her back to him, just like I coached her. She has on dark sunglasses, and from where he stands, I'm sure this asshat thinks Alice is Annie. I need him to think that for as long as possible.

"Whoa. I'm not sure what the problem is." The guy who's approached our table is a completely average, normal-looking man. For a minute, I wonder if this is an innocent mistake. But then I think of the odds of Annie seeing anyone she knows in this place at this time. There's no way. It's fucking him. He approached us and called her by name.

I look him over fast, trying to assess any vulnerabilities. The man's suit is cheap. I can tell by the way the stitches are pulling loose in some places. The dark gray fabric is pilling slightly by the right front pocket. He looks to be about fifty, maybe late fifties, and he's thin. I can't tell if he's carrying, but he looks meeker and shorter than I expected. If he has a gun, it's holstered under that shitty jacket. The man holds up his hands in surrender. "I thought I recognized my former coworker, Annie Hancock. I apologize if I'm mistaken."

"That's her," I tell him, never taking my eyes off the guy. I'm hoping like hell I get the details right. If he says he's Annie's former coworker, this can only be one man. The fuckstain law partner who asked her out after her dad sent her off to art school. I try to put the pieces together fast. Could this all be about a middle-aged man who was rejected for a single date? He's been stalking and harassing her because she ghosted him?

I've known men to do worse over less. But for now, I hang tight to my theories and press him to admit this is no accidental meeting.

"You know why we're here," I say. "This is no happy coincidence. You're telling me you didn't text her to arrange to meet here? In case you forgot, I'm the boyfriend. The tattooed, jerk-off boyfriend."

As I repeat the words of his text, his lips curl into a sneer. "Yeah, yeah, you are. And I do still hope you're not planning to be a hero today."

I'm trying to pay attention to the man in front of me when I hear Annie's voice in my ear. "Neveah is calling, Josh."

I nod slowly, angling the side of my head with the earpiece away from him. I just hope the guy in front of me thinks I'm focused on him. I hope Annie is careful.

If Neveah is in on this, she's got to be close. She may even be making sure that this fuck nugget is talking to her.

Out of the corner of my eye, I see a flash of neon yellow as Dog and Eagle move imperceptibly closer to us.

"So, what do you want?" I demand. "Or do you want to slip another little note under Annie's door like a pussy?"

His face burns red, and his nostrils flare. "Listen, cocksucker," he says, leaning a little closer to Alice's back. "I thought you agreed not to play the hero. You want things to get ugly, I'll make it ugly."

"You can't possibly be any uglier," I say. "Just looking at your face makes me sick, Engler."

When I say his name, he shakes his head. "Fucking jerk-off. My business is with Annie. You want to be a part of this, I'll make you a part of it."

"All I want to know is what you want from Annie," I tell him. "And I want you to leave her alone. So, what's that going to take?"

Alice sits there perfectly calm, but I see a slight tremble in the hands that she's tucked in her lap.

"Josh." Annie's voice crackles in my earpiece. "Don't let him leave. No matter what happens, don't let him leave the hotel."

I scratch my forehead and nod slightly, again hoping that Annie sees my signal.

"Why don't we have a talk, just me and you?" I nod at Engler. "Outside, away from all these nice people. Like men."

Engler shakes his head. "No, thanks. I don't need you to get me alone so you can try to beat my ass." He taps his right hip with a hand. "Again, I'm not here to cause trouble. You play nice, I'll play nice."

I hold up my hands now to show him I've got nothing in them. "I'll play nice. Why don't you tell us what you want, and then we can all go on our merry fucking way."

Engler nods slowly. "Annie—"

"No. Not her. You're talking to me." I take a step away from the table, and immediately Engler puts a hand under his jacket.

"I thought you said you were going to play nice," he hisses. "Keep your fucking hands where I can see them and take three steps away from Annie."

I shake my head. "Not going to do that. I'll keep my hands up, but if you take one step toward Annie, you're going to have to blast through both of us."

"Fuck you." Engler takes two steps back. "I can see you're not in any mood to talk, so I'll be on my way."

"Okay, okay… Calm down." For whatever reason, Annie said I can't let this guy leave. So, keeping him here is exactly what I'm going to do. "I'll calm down, you calm down. We both came all this way. Let's talk."

Engler throws a look over his shoulder and glares. I'm worried he's going to run, so I take a huge risk and sit. "I'm sitting," I say. "See? We're all good here. Now why don't you tell us what you want."

Engler twists his mouth into a frown. "You could do so much better than this piece of shit, Annie," he sneers.

"You could have had me."

He reaches out and touches Alice's ponytail. She sucks in a breath, and I lean forward in my chair, ready to fucking tear his arm off.

He just laughs. "That's all right. I've got myself bigger and better plans anyway."

Alice's shoulders tense, and I reach across the table to touch her arm.

"Babe, you're going to be all right." I hope the act is convincing. So far, he hasn't gotten a good look at Alice's face, and I'm worried what will happen the second he does. I also need to keep him from seeing my earpiece. I turn my glare on him. "Why don't you just tell us what you want, Engler? Unless what you want is a pen pal, because I don't think Annie's interested in getting any more little notes from you."

Engler's calm and cool as he shakes his head. "I just need a password," he says calmly. "And then I'll be on my way and our business here will be done."

Fuck. A password is not something Alice is going to be able to give him. And if he insists on talking to Alice, this whole little show blows wide open.

"What password do you want, and what do you need it for?" I ask, trying to stall for time.

"Listen, you stupid little fuck." Engler leans over Alice's shoulders and points at me. "This has nothing to do with you. Annie knows what her father owes me. She changed the password to our trust account the day she left the law firm. All I want is the password, and I'll be on my way."

In that moment, it's clear that he sees my earpiece. His mouth falls open, and he squints.

"You fucking piece of shit. I'm going to kill you."

Just as he makes a move for his jacket, I shout, "Dog!"

Alice dives under the table, and suddenly the place falls into chaos. Dog and Eagle pounce on the guy from behind, Dog punching him in the back of the head and Eagle holding down his legs so he can't move.

A security guard comes running and starts clearing people out of the lobby as I hear screaming. Engler is on the floor and blood is dripping from a nose that looks incredibly broken.

"You son of a bitch!" He flails against Eagle, who is holding down his legs like he's a rag doll. "I'm going to fucking kill you, and you...you bitch! Annie, you bitch! You're dead!"

Morris is on us in a second, helping his wife to her feet. When Engler sees Morris tower over him, he immediately falls silent. Morris bends over with a sick gleam in his eyes.

"Did I see you touch my wife, you filthy little piece of shit?"

Alice has pulled off the sunglasses, and tears are streaming from her eyes.

"I'm fine, babe," she says, wiping her cheeks. "He's nothing. It's over now."

Engler sees that Alice is not Annie, and he starts lurching and kicking. "You fucking bitch! You whore! Where's Annie? You whore!"

I can't stop what I fear is coming, and I'm not going to. I feel Annie beside me and I grab her arm, but she shakes me off. She tears the straw hat from her head and tosses it on the floor. The sunglasses are off, and I see a look in her sky-blue eyes that makes me proud.

"Can you get him up?" She's asking Dog and Eagle.

They haul his ass up from the floor, and he grunts like a prissy baby when they yank his arms.

Annie steps close to him and puts her finger in his face. "You're behind this? You've been stalking me at school all this time? You've known me since I was a child, Martin. What the fuck is wrong with you?"

Engler spits at her. "Fuck off, you worthless bitch. You're a talentless, spoiled princess. You and your shit father don't deserve anything. You stole it all from me."

I hear the sirens before I see the flashing lights. I look at my girl and know exactly what's coming. "If you're going to do it, babe…"

Annie lifts her dress, picks up her leg, and knees Engler in the nuts. He gasps and his knees drop from under him, but Dog and Eagle have him restrained, and they hold him up despite his wiggling. He coughs and gags, sputtering tendrils of saliva from his stupid lips.

"Martin, you are a worthless little bitch. I hope for every second of stress you've caused me, it comes back a hundredfold to you. Good luck in prison." She turns away from him just as two dozen plainclothes and uniformed cops descend on the lobby. Not far behind them is Neveah.

"Annie Hannie!" she screams over the noise of the crowd being cleared out. The officers serve Engler a warrant for his arrest and read him his rights.

I turn toward the sound of Neveah's voice just as

she clasps Annie in a hug. "Chick, you scared the ever-loving life out of me."

Annie says something into Neveah's ear, and they rock each other in a hug. Now that the cops have Engler, I turn to Morris.

"Thank you doesn't begin to cover it," I say.

He claps me on the shoulder and nods at Dog and Eagle, a shit-eating grin on his face. "I only wish I'd had a chance to get my hands on him before they took him away."

I thank the bikers for their role in this, and then, of course, the cops interview every single one of us about who we are and how we're involved. While the lobby of the hotel becomes a de facto crime scene, I confront the one person who I suspect has all the answers.

"You." I point a finger at Neveah. I stride through the bodies, stopping to hug Alice and thank her for her bravery. When I get over to Neveah, she smacks me on the shoulder.

"You almost outed me, you son of a gun." She's shaking her head. "I thought for sure you recognized me back in the dorms."

"I did," I say. "But I didn't want to give anything away until I knew exactly what side you were on."

I circle Annie's waist and pull her close. "You okay?"

She nods. "Never better."

Once I know my girl is okay, I turn to Neveah. "All right, spill it," I tell her. "There's no way this kind of police presence was for some jackass who wanted a password." I lift my brows. "Those cops had a warrant, which means they've been onto this asshat for some time."

"Yeah. Thank God the tracker was still in Annie's purse. And double thanks that she answered my call when I finally got her text." A huge grin takes over her face. "But before I explain, there's someone who wants to talk to Annie."

She steps aside, and a man who is about Engler's age comes running through the lobby. He practically skids on his dress shoes when he sees Annie.

"Dad." Annie takes off running, parting her way through the crowd of officers and the few remaining guests. "Dad." She practically jumps into his arms.

"How long have you been working for Mr. Hancock?" I ask.

Neveah grins. "About a year ago, Hancock discovered that Engler was working with a local rental firm. The rental agency was taking deposits from prospective renters on houses and apartments that weren't even available. Engler would contact the family and say he had a way to get them back some of their deposit and would charge them a flat fee for his 'legal services.' He'd contact his buddy at the rental agency, collect half the stolen deposit to give back to the family, and then he'd keep the amount that they'd pay in legal fees. Most of the time, the poor victims ended up losing the entire amount to that asshole." She shakes her head, a look of genuine disgust on her face. "Imagine being out thousands for a security deposit and first month's rent, giving notice on your place, and then finding out you'd been scammed? Engler would get them half their money back but then keep it in legal fees. Some of these people were left on the street, man. Shady piece of low-life shit."

"And Hancock found out?" I ask. Annie is hugging Alice, who was talking now with her father.

Neveah nods. "Rental fraud, mail fraud, and bank fraud. There was a mingling of funds between legit law firm business and this scam. Hancock had nothing to do with it, so he contacted law enforcement and has been working with them for over a year to gather enough evidence to bring down both Engler and his associates at the rental agency."

"So, you're law enforcement now?" I ask, curious how the pink buns and art school weigh into all that.

"Nah." Neveah laughs. "And I'm no artist either, man. And I'm still independent. Mr. Hancock hired me to look out for Annie. The cops working with him to bring Engler down didn't see a threat to Annie, so they wouldn't put her under any kind of protection. Hancock wasn't taking any chances. He figured when the shit went down, his daughter needed to be far away from all of it. The man put up a lot of money to make sure Annie got into art school and that I was assigned to be her RA to keep tabs on her." She clapped her hands. "That was the most fun I've had on a job ever, man. I'm the shittiest artist on the planet. Drove that June Crossard lady fucking nuts."

I nod, the pieces starting to fall into place. "So, you're the one who put all the trackers on Annie?"

She nods. "Had to know where my client was at all times. You sure as fuck didn't make things easy on me."

I have more questions, but she gives me a playful smack on the arm.

"What about you?" she asks. "This whole boyfriend-girlfriend act over now? Because I think Annie's about to introduce you to Daddy."

I roll my shoulders and pull out my earpiece. "It's no act," I tell her. "It didn't start out that way, but now it's real."

She nods and gives me a grin. "Well, good luck. Now, forget my face, would ya? Maybe I'll run into you someplace sometime. And if I do, you don't know me."

"Annie's going to miss you, I think," I tell her. "She considered you a real friend."

Neveah gives me a small smile. "Hazard of the job. Good thing you don't have to break her heart too."

She wanders through the crowd, stopping to shake Mr. Hancock's hand, and then she's gone.

I have no intention of leaving Annie. Not now. Not ever.

In the chaos of the red and blue lights, the conversations of the officers, and the loud voices of the bikers, I turn and prepare to meet Annie's dad.

CHAPTER 19
ANNIE

BETWEEN MY FATHER, Neveah, and the really nice officers who sat down and took my statement, I finally feel like I have answers.

They still haven't charged the custodian at the school who stole my keys, ransacked my room, and left me the threatening notes that Engler paid him to leave, but they have him in custody and are questioning him.

As far as I know, within the next few days, this whole mess will be behind me.

Martin Engler must have figured out that my dad was onto him. It seems like he wanted the password to my father's trust account so he could clear it out and run before he was arrested on so many counts of fraud, I lost count. My father told me everything. That he paid my way into art school and hired Neveah to keep me safe. Turns out, I'd had security all along. I just didn't know it.

Thankfully, when I'd told Neveah about the notes, she'd realized something had changed and that Engler was about to make a move. The cops got their warrant and were ready to close in on him. The fact that he threatened to kill me is recorded on Josh's glasses cam. If they can use the video as evidence, maybe that'll ensure Engler spends even longer in prison.

Jerk.

I'll bet when he asked me to dinner that night, he wanted to find out what I knew about his little side operation. Or maybe he was going to try to get the password out of me then. I feel almost sick thinking what desperate measures he might have gone to if I actually had gone to dinner with him that night. This story might not have had such a happy ending.

By the time the hotel lobby clears out of most of the law enforcement personnel, I'm exhausted and starving. I kiss my father goodbye.

"You coming home tonight, honey?" he asks, looking at Josh. "We're safe now. You can go back to school, come home…anything you want. We're both free."

"And broke," I remind him. "I can't believe how much you spent to protect me, Dad." He hasn't told me how much it cost, but when he told me what he did, I immediately felt sick. I'm sure Dad spent all his savings and dipped into his retirement to make sure I was not hurt by the investigation into Engler.

"Annie." My dad reaches for my cheek and holds my face with one hand. "You are the most important thing to me in the entire world. I don't need money if I don't have you. And if I didn't have you, money would mean nothing. I'll earn it back. You're safe. You're here, and that's all that matters."

My father reaches out a hand to Josh. "Send me your bill," he says. "I'll take care of your expenses and all your time."

I look to Josh, relieved that he won't be out the money he's spent on not working for other clients because he's been with me, but Josh shakes his head.

"Thank you for the offer, Mr. Hancock. But I wouldn't take your money. Not for this. Not for her." Josh shakes my father's hand and then turns to me. "Do you want to go home with your father, babe?"

The way he says "babe" sends my heart into a frenzy. I lace my fingers through his. "What I really want is some dinner and maybe to watch some baking shows."

He tightens his fingers around mine. "Tiny." Josh's voice carries over the sounds of the diminishing crowd. The massive man lumbers over to us and claps Josh on the shoulder.

"Yo, what's up, Arrow?" He nods to my father, and my father reaches out a hand and introduces himself.

"Thank you for giving my daughter a place to stay when she had no place else to go." Dad motions to me. "Honey, give me Tiny's contact information. If you ever need a real estate attorney, I'm happy to help you in any way I can."

"Yeah? We've been working with this attorney we call Fingers. I don't know if you know him…"

Tiny and my father turn to walk away when Josh

calls after him, "We'll clear out of Crow's room tonight, man."

Tiny waves a hand. "Stay as long as you need. He ain't using it."

Josh turns back to me. "One more night with the bikers?"

I give him a smile. "On one condition."

I'm about to say it, but Josh gets the words out first. "Pancake Circus?"

If I didn't know it before, I'm sure now. I just might be falling in love with Josh.

By the time we say our goodbyes and another round of thank-yous to Dog, Eagle, Morris, and Alice, I'm way too tired for Pancake Circus. And those are words I never thought I'd say.

We climb into Josh's truck and pick up fast-food burgers, which we eat on the drive back to the compound.

"What's next, babe?" he asks, reaching across the seat for my hand. "You should be safe if you want to go back to school."

I nod, thinking the question over. "I'm not sure, to be honest. I have a lot to think about." I trail my fingertips over his strong hand. "Josh," I say, growing serious, "we were in real danger tonight. Engler had a gun under his jacket."

I see Josh's jaw muscles clench through the soft brown hairs of his scruff. His lips are tight. "I know he did," he says. "But we're safe now."

"But you do this for a living," I remind him. "Have you been in this kind of danger before?"

He tightens his fingers around mine. "Yeah, Annie. I have."

We're both silent then. I'm not sure what to say. I have no right to ask him to change his life or his career for me, and yet I can't help wondering whether he would if I did.

When we finally arrive at the compound, the place is lit up like Christmas. Tiny, Dog, and Eagle are in the kitchen, smoking cigars and reliving the night. They have drinks, and they look like they've been having some kind of fun.

When we get inside, Dog roars out Josh's name. "Arrow, you sonofabitch!"

He steamrolls over to us in a cloud of cigar smoke and practically lifts Josh off his feet with a rowdy hug. I can't help grinning. These bikers are everything I expected them to be and somehow more.

Tiny jerks his thumb toward the back part of the compound, where Crow's room is. "Take a load off till tomorrow. You got someplace better you'd rather be?" he asks.

Josh looks at me, and I shake my head. "Thank you all again so, so much."

The guys take turns giving me hugs, and then Josh and I head back to Crow's room.

Once we're inside, Josh locks the door, and I start to peel off my clothes.

"I'm dying for a shower," I say. "All I can feel is Martin Engler's eyes all over me."

"Go on, then," he says. "Take your time. I'm going to go talk to Tiny. Meet you back here."

In the shower, I spend maybe too long feeling down about everything. About losing Neveah as a friend. I don't know if she plans to keep in touch now that she's no longer my RA. I guess she was never really an art student. I'll miss her, but what's even more, I'll miss the fact that I thought I finally had my life on track. I feel lost. Directionless.

I wash my hair and try to console myself that I'm safe. I don't have to figure anything out tonight. All I need to do is take things one day at a time. But I think the reality that I really was in danger, still hasn't fully hit me.

I climb out of the shower and pull on my pajamas soaking wet. I run back to the bedroom and close myself inside.

I sit on the end of the bed, shaking, just thinking about the times when someone knew where I was and what I was doing. Some custodian gave a stranger access to me in exchange for money. I am still sitting on the edge of the bed trembling when Josh comes back into the bedroom.

He must have grabbed a shower after he talked to Tiny because he's towel-drying his hair. He's shirtless and wearing a pair of basketball shorts that I haven't seen before.

The minute he's inside the room, he locks the door and sits beside me. "Annie," he says gently. "You're soaking wet. What happened?"

"I got out of the shower. I didn't put on lotion. I didn't dry myself. I…"

The words come out fast, and it's almost as if I'm

freezing. My lips are trembling with something like ice-cold fear.

"Baby," he says. "I'm going to take care of you, okay?"

He pulls the towel from around his shoulders and uses it to blot my hair dry. He takes clumps in his hands and dries it so gently, it's as if he's done this a million times.

"Stand for me, Annie." I do what he says, and he unbuttons my pajamas and tugs off my shorts. "As much as I want this to be good for you, I'm really struggling seeing you like this, babe."

I look down and realize his dick is so hard it's tenting the front of his basketball shorts. I start to giggle, and then I completely lose it. I fall back on the bed, laughing, completely naked, and Josh just shakes his head.

"Do you have lotion?" he asks. "You're dry, but you said you didn't moisturize. We can't let you go to sleep with dry skin, babe."

Now that I'm dry and starting to calm down, the jitters have passed. I'm naked and laughing with the person I most want to be with in the world. Josh is hard, the television is on, and if I ask nicely, I bet he'll rub my body lotion anywhere I want.

I'm going to be okay. Life is a mess, and my future is uncertain, but I have my father. I have my safety. I have Josh.

"Lotion and condoms," I remind him.

Josh claps his hands. "That's literally my favorite combination."

I grab a bottle of moisturizer from the toiletries I've packed and hand him the bottle. "Where do you want to start?" I ask.

He grabs my foot and tickles the bottom with his fingers. I squeal and pull away. "Hell no. Not there."

"Okay, okay." He points to the bed, and I lie on my back. But he shakes his head, sexy grin on his face. "Babe, come on. The ass king is holding a bottle of lotion." He makes a roll-over movement with his hand, and I obey.

I close my eyes and settle in just as I feel the ice-cold squirt of cream fall onto the back of my right calf. I squeal at the cold, but then his strong hands encircle my leg, massaging the lotion into my skin with firm strokes.

"Annie," he says, kneading deep into my muscles.

"Can't talk…" My eyes are half closed and my mouth half open. I'm so relaxed already, I might start drooling on the bed. "Feels too good," I mumble.

Josh laughs, and I feel the featherlight pressure of his lips as he kisses my butt cheek. "Just you wait, babe."

"What were you going to say?" I mouth the words against the blanket.

"It can wait." His voice is thick and gruff, and all sound disappears as he works his way up the backs of my legs. He squirts me with another pump of ice-cold lotion, and the heat of his hands against the contrast of the chilly lotion brings every hair on my body on end.

I feel alive and delicious. I part my legs a bit, giving him access to my inner thighs. He kneads his way through the tight muscles, and the tension leaves my body. He massages my left leg, putting as much attention into this one as my right. By the time I feel his hot hands cup my ass, I'm so relaxed, I'm nearly asleep.

But I wake right up when I feel him settle between my legs. He nudges my knees farther apart, and I feel his breaths teasing my inner thighs.

"Do you like being licked?" he asks.

I grunt, too relaxed and happy to form a word.

He chuckles and then slips his hands under my hips and lifts my body just a little bit so his tongue can reach my pussy.

"Fuck," I say, able to form that word as I feel his tongue against my wet lips. My pussy throbs in anticipation, but his licks are light and tentative, like he's trying to taste his way around every inch. When he slips just the tip of his tongue a little deeper, into my wet heat, my legs jerk in surprise.

"Good?" he asks.

"So good," I assure him, lifting my ass a bit to give him better access.

He dips his tongue inside me, but he avoids my clit, which leaves me aroused but desperate for him. I lift my ass higher, but I stop when I feel a very slippery finger slip between my cheeks.

"I'm just going to touch you, babe," he warns. "Tell me if it's too much."

I'm not sure what too much will feel like, but I don't have to wonder for long. Josh's mouth is gone from my pussy, but I feel his fingertip push against my other opening.

The pressure is interesting and not pleasurable, but not uncomfortable.

When I feel him push harder, slipping just the tip of a finger inside my ass, I clench up involuntarily.

"Relax, babe," he whispers. "Just lean into it. I won't hurt you."

And he doesn't. As one fingertip penetrates my ass, he uses a different finger to stroke my pussy. The pleasure of his touch on my clit contrasts against the tight pressure in my ass, making me feel so many sensations at once, I can't think straight. I'm aroused and want more, but I don't know what I want more of.

I rock my hips, trying to bring him closer, deeper, something, when finally he says, "Flip over. I want your tits."

While I settle onto my back, Josh squirts lotion onto his hands and uses his damp bath towel to wipe his fingers clean. Then he climbs onto the bed and kisses his way up my calves, thighs, and stomach.

By the time he reaches my breasts, I am aching with need for him. I feel empty where I want to feel full, and my nipples throb in anticipation. I cup my breasts, trying to ease the nearly painful arousal.

He watches me, fire in his eyes as I touch myself. He strokes his cock, thick and hard, and then, as if remembering, he gets up and grabs the last two condoms from the top of the dresser. "We're going to need both," he promises.

As he sucks my nipples, I stroke his hair and pull his face closer to my frantically beating heart. "You're the best fake boyfriend I've ever had," I whisper.

He lifts his face and looks at me, then looks down at my bare chest. He pinches one of my nipples between two fingers, and I suck air at the glorious electricity that floods my body.

"This feels pretty real to me," he says. "You think this is fake?"

He settles himself between my legs, and I grab a condom, practically dropping it in my rush to tear it open. I hand the coiled circle to him, and I watch as he sheathes his rock-hard length.

"Josh," I say, reaching between us and guiding his cock toward me.

He doesn't tease me this time. There's no start and stop, no milking and toying. He slides himself fully inside me with one deep thrust.

I gasp and wrap my arms around him, fanning my hands along the muscles of his back. He feels so good, so hot and strong and perfect.

"There's nothing fake about this," I tell him, wrapping my legs around his waist.

He grips my hips with his hands and crushes my lips with his. "Be mine, Annie. I want you when we don't have to hide in this room. I want you in my bed and my home and my life. Yeah?"

"Add heart to that, and you have a deal." I pant the words between every thrust.

He breathes a single word against my lips. "Deal."

EPILOGUE

ARROW

SIX MONTHS LATER...

"Babe?" I carry a cup of coffee up to our bedroom. I've been up since dawn and have already had enough coffee to float out to sea. The room is dark and quiet thanks to the blackout drapes Annie installed, and only the soft sounds of Annie's breathing filling the room.

I set the coffee on the bedside table. As my eyes adjust to the dark, I stroke her hair.

"Babe," I say quietly. "I gotta roll."

She mumbles something softly in her sleep, but I feel a hand reach out to clasp my thigh. "Morning, baby."

I lean down and kiss her hair. "Your coffee's here. I gotta roll. I'm working a half day, so I'll see you by noon."

I'm standing up when she tightens her fingers against my stiff work pants. "Kiss," she whispers. She thrashes against the blankets and sits up.

I reach for her neck and draw her close. I hold her, the warmth of her body making me wish I could strip off my steel-toe boots and wake her up properly. With my mouth and my already-firm dick.

But I've got a new job, and the work won't wait. So, I give her a kiss and hold her tight.

"I'm so proud of you, babe," I tell her. "You're going to be great today. I can't wait to see you."

"Josh?" Her voice is sleepy, but her eyes are open. "I love you."

"Love you too."

I leave her and her coffee and head out to the truck. I'm just pulling out of the driveway when I get a call from Tiny.

"Yo," he says in greeting.

"Hey, man. What's up?" I check the time on the dashboard. It's half past five, and I'm not due to the house for another half hour. I'm a solid twenty minutes away, so if Tiny needs something, he'd better get out with it.

"Good news, bad news."

I can hear Tiny slurping something through a straw, and I shake my head, a slight grin on my face. Marla, his friend, has him hooked on smoothies. It's a healthier habit than Coke, but still. I'd rather not hear how healthy he's trying to be.

"So, Hancock drew up some paperwork. We've got three more houses you need to look at today. You want to fit those in and skip the Redfern Lane place? I know you're working a half day, or I'd have you do it all."

I mentally calculate the time it'll take to run out to Annie's dad's law office. Since Engler was arrested,

Annie's dad decided to start buying houses and flipping them as a way to begin to earn back some of the cash he lost. Since my good buddies Tiny, Crow, and Morris are dabbling in contracting, they've all been working together on scouting flips and getting the work done.

Turns out, Annie's dad has friends in real estate who've been feeding him leads on fixer-uppers. The business was running so smoothly, I approached Morris about coming on board.

I have no background in construction, but I wasn't able to afford to renew the lease. Morris came through with an offer to teach me their business, starting off with the easy stuff. I've been taking classes at night to learn home inspections, so I'm the first guy on-site before we put in an offer on a house. Tiny, Crow, and some of the other guys have been helping me learn the ropes, but it turns out all my years of having no money and taking odd jobs have paid off. I know a lot more about construction than I thought, and I have a good eye for estimating.

Annie was more than happy to see me leave investigations. I introduced Neveah to all my old contacts, and every time she gets a job from one of them, she kicks me back a couple bucks. It's nothing big, but over the months, the referral fees have kept me and Annie in touch with Neveah. Since I'm no longer in the business, Annie and Neveah have been able to stay friends without Neveah worrying about me blowing her cover. It's been a win-win.

"Yeah," I tell Tiny, calculating the distance between

the addresses he's rattled off. "Is anyone meeting me today?"

"You're on your own today, man. Just take pics and upload them to the system. I'll sign off if you do, and we'll have three more new jobs if all goes well."

"See you later at the opening?" I ask before we go back to our days.

"Wouldn't miss it." Without so much as a goodbye, Tiny hangs up.

I punch an address into my GPS and head to the east side of town. Three new houses to flip means months of work for the crew. Profit for Annie's dad. And job stability for me.

I never thought I'd have a career or an education. But I'm working on all that shit and more. I'm thinking about what it might be like to have a wife. I know everybody says you've got to know someone at least six months before you know them.

I call bullshit on that.

Annie moved in to my condo immediately after we cleared out of Crow's room at the compound. She fit in my home as easily as she fit in my bed. Nothing in my life has ever been as easy as it is with Annie. If Carlene from Pancake Circus had her way, we'd already be married, but we got off to such a fast start, I don't want to rush any moment of the time I have with her.

We have forever ahead of us. I'm damn sure of that, and I know she feels the same way. I don't want to waste a day. But that doesn't mean I don't want to take every step and savor it.

We have a lot to save for, a lot to plan for. Annie has

big dreams, and right now, we're sinking every penny we make into my education and her business. A ring and fancy party—that'll come in time.

For now, I make the turns my GPS guides me to, and I realize how much my life has changed. I'm not chasing shadows anymore. I'm not hiding from the light, trying to keep the bad guys from putting one over on the good ones. And for the first time in a long time, I'm feeling at ease.

I'm happy.

ANNIE

I stare in the bathroom mirror and put the slightest bit of makeup around my eyes. I'm fresh from the shower, hair almost air-dried, wearing nothing but a contented smile. I shake my head as I see the tiniest little bruise on the side of my boob. Josh and his damn teeth. They feel so good in the moment, but sometimes our sexy times leave a mark. I touch the tiny discoloration, and a stupid, love-sick grin covers my face.

Who can blame me?

My sexy PI is no longer a PI. He's just my sexy baby now. I've wondered about whether the day will come when I might become Annie Aronowicz. That's a mouthful, to be sure. But if that becomes my name someday, it's a name I'll say with pride.

I pull on a light sweater and a flowy skirt with a pair of ankle boots, then get ready to hit the road. Today is a day I've been working toward for six months.

After Engler was arrested, I spent a couple days

trying to figure out what to do. I met with June Crossard, my adviser, for some honest talks. She told me the truth. That if my father hadn't paid my way into art school, I probably would never have been accepted.

"You have skills, Annie," she said, that severe face of hers pinched as though it hurt her to say the words. "But skills aren't vision. Skills aren't passion. Skills can make up for talent, but only to a point."

I'd sat in her office and taken it all in. She's an artist who's shown in galleries. She's had work written up, reviewed. She was once paid six figures for a commission that apparently is the centerpiece of an office building in Denmark.

June Crossard was trying to soften the blow, but I understood what she was saying. If I wanted to be an artist, I'd have a lot of work to do, yes, but even more than that, I'd have to do some serious soul-searching.

"Let me ask you this." June leaned back in her chair and just looked at me. "How badly do you want it? That's what this all comes down to. If you want this more than anything in the world, then nothing—not what I say, not a degree—nothing should matter. So, tell me, Annie, what do you want more than anything?"

I didn't even have to think about the answer. All the months of questioning myself and wondering what my message and vision and future were came down to this. And I made my decision. I quit school. I spent a month figuring out what came next. I knew I didn't want to go back to work for my dad. Even when Josh started working construction gigs and flipping houses with my dad and the bikers. I knew I wanted to forge my own future.

A future that I made with my own two hands.

Josh did some security consulting for the school, and in exchange, they refunded almost all the tuition my father had paid.

Dad wouldn't let me give him the money back. The school paid it back to him, but he turned around and wrote a check to Morris and Alice, paying in advance for the security deposit and several months' rent on Josh's office.

Then I got to work. And today, that work is coming to fruition.

I jump into my car with a smile on my face. I check my phone and it's blowing up with texts, but I don't answer them. I want a few minutes to myself before things get crazy.

So many years ago, I lost my mother. I wonder if she would have been here today to support me. If she would have liked Josh. I know the answers to those questions. She would have loved Josh. I mean, everyone loves Josh. No one more than me, but that's expected.

Maybe Carlene. She's been trying to get the cooks over at Pancake Circus to make a specialty plate just for him. I giggle. I'm lucky to have people like her in my life. I'm sure if my mom were here, she would be with me right now, cheering me on. Maybe in some ways, she is.

When I pull into the strip mall, it's a little before noon. Everything is set, so all I have to do is open. I get out of my car and unlock the door that was once Josh's office. Now, it's a completely refurbished retail space—Annie's Artscape.

I'm only inside a minute when the door flies open behind me.

"Annie." Alice has two dozen helium balloons, one bunch in each hand. "I'm so glad you're here."

She kisses my cheek and hands over the balloons. "Rider has been crying for one of these all morning." She rolls her eyes. "I should have known to get some balloons just for him."

"He can have them," I say, offering a whole bunch back to Alice.

She shakes her head. "Lia says the balloons will freak out the dogs." Alice winks. "I'll get him set up with crafts, and he'll be just fine."

Alice looks around the space, a happy smile on her face. "It looks so, so good. Are you ready?"

Annie's Artscape will be open for small classes, private studio space, anything that anyone with a passion to create can imagine. We have a colorful table and small chairs up front where kids can work, and Josh's former office has a long table where adults can work with textiles or pencils, crochet, knit, or model with clay. I have paints, reclaimed materials, and more colored pencils and pens than should be legal in one space.

When I open the doors for business today at noon, I'm hoping that the community comes in and finds their joy in making things. I already have three after-school classes fully paid and booked, and I have a moms-only morning adult coloring class that starts next week. Lia is offering a discount to customers who drop their dogs off at the day care while they're at my studio.

I don't have time to get emotional. I nod to Alice, tears of joy wetting my lashes, when all of a sudden, the place fills up. Tiny and Marla are first to arrive, carrying Rider, who is crying and reaching out for the balloons. Morris joins next, kissing his wife and promising to bring Zoey and their baby by after school. Dog and Eagle show up in their neon-yellow construction shirts.

"Where's the asshole?" Dog asks.

"I'm right here, you fucker." Josh is holding the door open for Neveah, who is carrying a huge bouquet of flowers.

"Love what you've done with the place, Annie Hannie," she says, giving me a kiss. She walks through the space, looking over the fabrics and supplies, admiring the work we've done. "This place makes me want to take up art." She winks at me, then says her goodbyes since she's surveilling something and has places to be.

Leo and Tim stop by to congratulate us before heading back to their shop. And then, last but not least, I see the man who made all this possible.

"Dad." I meet him at the door. He's standing outside, soaking it all in. He's been here so many times during the renovation, but he's looking at my name on the door like it's the first time he's seen it.

"I'm so, so proud of you, Annie." He doesn't move. Doesn't say anything. Just wipes at his eyes with a fingertip. "So proud. Are you happy?"

I may not have a message or a vision for my art. I

may not have a fancy degree or a gallery showing. But I have passion, and I've found a way to express it.

"I have never been happier," I assure my dad. "Now, come on in."

While my dad chats up Morris, Josh comes over and pulls me close to his chest.

"My baby's big day," he breathes against my hair. "Congratulations, baby."

I look up at him. "Who'd have thought. Can you imagine what my life might have turned out like if I'd hired one of those other PIs? Thank goodness none of them was even half as hot as you."

He laughs and gives my ass a light spank, trying to be discreet so no one else can see. "We've all ended up where we were meant to be," he says.

And even though it wasn't easy getting here, I know he's right.

This is right.

We're right.

And I'm so, so happy that this is not the end of our story.

It's just the beginning.

Want to know more about Crow, Morris, and the gang? Read **FLAME for FREE**, Men of Inked: Heatwave Book 1 and start your next favorite series.

>> Read FLAME for FREE <<

Could you love a man surrounded by danger?

Gigi Gallo's childhood was filled with the roar of a motorcycle and the hum of a tattoo gun. Fresh out of college, she's about to start working at her family's tattoo studio — Inked. But when she showed up the first day, she never expected to run into someone tall, dark, and totally sexy from her not-so-innocent past.

Pike Moore is a bossy biker with a cocky attitude and an even bigger ego. He came to Inked to start over. New town. New job. New roots. None of that included coming face-to-face with the hot chick who spent a week in his bed before she vanished without a trace.

But when Pike's dark family history catches up with him, can he stop Gigi from being caught in the crossfire?

Download the FLAME eBook for FREE at
menofinked.com/flame

>> Download Throttle Me for FREE <<

LOVE SIGNED PAPERBACKS?

Visit *chelleblissromance.com* for signed paperbacks and book merchandise.

Don't Miss Out!

Join my newsletter for exclusive content, special freebies, and so much more. Click here to get on the list or visit **menofinked.com/news**

Do you want to have your very own **SIGNED paperbacks** on your bookshelf? Now you can get them! Tap here to check out Chelle Bliss Romance or visit **chelleblissromance.com** and stock up on paperbacks, Inked gear, and other book worm merchandise!

Join over 10,000 readers on Facebook in Chelle Bliss Books private reader group and talk books and all things reading. Tap here to come be part of the family or visit **facebook.com/groups/blisshangout**

Want to be the first to know about upcoming sales and new releases? Follow me on Bookbub or visit bookbub. com/authors/chelle-bliss

Made in United States
North Haven, CT
02 August 2024

55676282R00178